REVENGE
THE ASSASSIN

--- PULLING THREADS ---

Book Fourteen

SHERYLL O'BRIEN

This is a work of fiction. All characters in this book are the product of an overactive imagination. Any businesses, organizations, places, events, and incidents are used fictionally. Any resemblance to a real person, living or dead, is a tremendous coincidence.

ISBN 978-1-939351-37-1

Printed in United States of America

Mom,

On October 9, 2020, Bullet Bungalow was published. This was my dedication.

To my mother, Ruth Shirley Bodreau. Thank you for not saying – to my face – everything you surely must be thinking. I love you mieces to pieces – whatever the hell that means.

I know what it means, Mom.

ACKNOWLEDGMENT

As we inch toward the final Pulling Threads story, I would like to thank the wonderful characters who have kept me on my toes, surprised me on every step of the journey, and have settled in my heart.

A particular shout out to John Maxwell, the Annoying One, and Rocco Fiancetti, the Kitschy One, and Malcolm Price, **The One**. Thank you for your strength and stamina—in and out of bed, and in showers, and on airplanes, and in conference rooms, and countless places, near and far.

A heartfelt thank you to my team:

Andria Flores ~ Editor extraordinaire.
Nancy Pendleton ~ Goddess of the publishing world.
Jessica Champion ~ Web designer and manager.
25 Hours Consulting

A special thanks:

To my wonderful family and friends who have called, texted, and emailed—who have taken to social media with thumbs up and words of love and support—who have turned the pages of a Pulling Threads book—my heartfelt appreciation. And to those who have yet to do any of those things—get busy!

Testimonials

--- Pulling Threads ---

Bullet Bungalow
Netti Barn
Cutters Cove
They Run
They Hide
They Choose

PENOBSCOT BAY
A Rocco Fiancetti Incorporated Investigation

Reasons
Rescues
Resolutions
Torment
Tango
Tests
Resolve
Revenge

Coming soon…

Rebound

--- Twisted Threads ---

Her Scream

Coming soon…

Stay Safe

Christmas Wish List

Domination

Children

Freedom

REVENGE

Revenge

Christmas

Rocco Fiancetti checks the clock in the great room, pulls a deep breath and quietly moves away from the few holiday stragglers milling about. He finds his wife and kisses her cheek, "It's nearly midnight, mi amore."

She smiles and runs her fingertips down his arm, finding his hand for a reassuring squeeze before he leaves. "I'll start the fire in the suite."

He smiles, though it doesn't warm his eyes. "Midnight," he reminds himself, or maybe admonishes himself, as he moves swiftly down a set of stairs and along a dimly lit corridor, the one he should have traveled long before now. It's Christmas, after all, and he has a son, who should have received a visit from his father—**on** Christmas.

Rocco stands at the doorway to the medical suite waiting for the final minutes of the day to tick past. "No," he answers the silent question. "The day did not slip away." The shake of his head accompanies his next whisper. "No. Staying away from my son was not easy, it was unbearable." He slumps against the doorjamb, exhaustion burning deep. He offers a confession, perhaps a concession. "The beast of revenge is my constant companion now. It has reared its ugly head and demands sustenance—a pound of flesh, an eye for an eye. The beast is not welcome at my son's bedside, not on Christmas." An alarm vibrates on his watch, "Midnight. My vow has been honored." Rocco drags his heavy load to the bedside chair hoping it will support the weight of a man and the beast that lives deep within…

Casella, Italy
1989

Rocco and Eleni married the day they learned she was with child. The newlyweds traipsed the Italian Riviera celebrating their love along the crescent shaped Mediterranean coastline. The turquoise inlets of Portofino, Porto Venere, Venazza and Rapallo captured the young woman's heart and unleashed the young artist's creativity.

"Rocco Fiancetti, you are a master like your father. Your work is so truly yours. It is exquisite," Eleni declared.

"You are exquisite, Eleni, in every way," he touched the place where she nurtured their creation.

The young lovers heeded the advice of Rocco's father and searched for artistic wonders in the rugged terrain and pastel seaside towns, and not in the museums and galleries that beckoned her visit.

"Stay far from places that draw the scrutiny of those who search for Eleni. I have met her father's henchman—he is driven to find her," **Lorenzo Fiancetti warned.**

The couple happily complied with that directive, and as he'd promised before leaving Genoa, Rocco made regular calls home and shared joys and concerns about his pregnant wife. "Papa, Eleni wearies of travel and tires easily."

"She is nearing six months, Rocco, she needs to take root. Travel to the stone cottage of your uncle. He will come and settle you there. Share your first Christmas, then welcome your baby after the New Year. Andros Karras can rip his daughter from a lover's arms, but he cannot take a wife from her husband or a mother from her child."

The weary travelers made their way to the mountainous village of Casella northeast of Genoa arriving only days before Christmas. They were met at the narrow-gauge railway station by Cepriano Batista.

"Rocco," Cepriano crooned, his near black eyes hooded with worry for the young man he considered a son.

"Uncle." The men kissed cheeks, slapped shoulders, and pulled one another in for several hugs. "Let me introduce my wife, Eleni."

Cepriano's charm-dimples cut deep, and his eyes abandoned worry when he stared upon his nephew's prize, "Eleni, such beauty should be celebrated. Rocco you must sketch this woman while your child nestles deep."

Eleni laughed, "Senor Batista, Rocco suggests use of your stone cottage is for my respite. He does not say he tires of dragging sketch pads full of my image."

Cepriano loved Eleni already, "Come. The cottage is a walk."

The men settled Eleni then made a trip to the village square for provisions. Cepriano wasted no time issuing his warning, "Andros Karras will not rest until he finds her, Rocco. He is a ruthless man. Pay heed to this."

"Will we be safe here?"

"Si. I pay heavily for privacy in Casella. The villagers will hold their tongues. It is the transients who will bring trouble and darken your doorstep with it. Stay until the birth, then come to Genoa, or go to London. Your mother has the resources to protect you."

"I want nothing of that world."

"Your ideas will change when you have your child."

Joy Fiancetti joins Rocco at Manuel's bedside. "I disturbed you."

Rocco takes the hand that rests on his shoulder and kisses it, "Mi, amore, you disturbed my heart the moment I found you."

Joy smiles. Sort of. "Manuel is turning the corner. He looks like your son, again."

"Si. He is fighting like my son again. He is refusing sedatives and pulling himself free of their insidious hold." Rocco becomes quiet for a moment. "Manuel calls her name. He knows Leavy is in peril. Her absence will demand his freedom from this bed."

Joy touches Rocco's shoulder again, "When you're done, please join me at the Computer Center. There is a situation."

Memories lift through the fog.

Felicity Ferraro's head is throbbing. Thoughts swirl. Words bang. His words … their words…

"Felicity. It's about time you joined me."

"Mathis, I mean Mr. Reynolds, what … how … what?"

The physically fit, impeccably dressed, handsome man of fifty walked to her, "You need better security. Make sure you get it. I want to be protected when I visit." He ran his fingers through the damp ends of her hair, moved the terry cloth robe off one of her shoulders.

She blocked his hand, "I'm married."

"No, Felicity, you're widowed."

She passed out before hearing anything more.

The ice cold woman rouses from her fainting spell to find she's in her own bed. Her comforter is pulled to her shoulders, yet shivers have taken hold, 'death shivers' her Irish nana used to call them. In this case the name aptly fits. Felicity rolls to the side when she senses she is not alone. A pain shoots through her head, shoots again when she touches an egg that has formed on her skull.

"You fainted."

Felicity wills her eyes to focus on the man standing at the foot of her bed, "Mr. Reynolds?"

"Mathis. You are allowed to call me Mathis."

Felicity touches her head again this time avoiding the egg. She welcomes her clearing vision—damns her clearing thoughts. "Paul is dead?" she whispers.

"He is."

Somehow, Felicity lunges the length of the bed tumbles off its end and stumbles against the man who pulls the enraged woman close. "Do you know what you've done?" she screams.

"Calm down, Felicity."

"Calm down? Calm down! I'll never see my children again. Paul knows where they are. Paul knows…" Felicity collapses into the arms of her husband's executioner.

Mathis lets the rage tears flow fast and furious against his chest. When the storm passes and there is nothing left in the depleted woman, he holds her upright and states flatly, "I know where your children are. All of your children, Felicity. Lie down."

Memories lift through the fog…

"Mrs. Ferraro, this is Mathis Reynolds, I believe you know me by my preferred title, The Body."

The head of The Realm set his expectations, then disconnected their call. She was still holding the phone in her trembling hand when she received a text. It contained a video of her four-year-old twins sitting on a rock at the water's edge, surrounded by a lush forest. The tykes were dressed for a day of woodland exploring with little binoculars hanging from their necks, and wide-brimmed hats covering their heads. Rainboots with cartoon frogs and turtles showed signs of recent water play. The boy and girl were holding their tiny hands in the air and waving to the camera, their little singsong voices calling out, "Hi, Mommy. We love you."

~

The Body disconnected their call. Immediately after, Felicity received a video text. This time her twins were moving back and forth on swings affixed to a thick tree branch, their tiny bottoms barely causing a bend in the black rubber seats, and their kicking legs pumped off-rhythm. They squealed in delight as they sang, "Push, please, high, high."

The nauseated woman tries to move toward the bed; she sways against him. The feel of the mattress against the back of her thighs steadies her, just enough. She drops onto it, crawls into place and pulls the comforter from his hands. She covers herself then clutches the downy fabric between her fingers to keep the cover taught at her neck.

He sits on the edge of her bed and pulls his cell from his pocket. In seconds Felicity hears the voices of her children, all four of them. In chorus they wish, "Merry Christmas, Mommy."

Her world spins from its axis once again.

Darkness has already filled the four corners of her room when Felicity awakens. Before she registers the time and space around her, an unpleasantness assaults from within. Her hand goes to her head, to her stomach, to her mouth. She pushes herself from bed, stumbles to the bathroom and throws herself against the cold porcelain of the toilet. She retches heartily.

"I'm afraid you have a mild concussion," Mathis says from behind.

Felicity follows the voice, finds him, the leader of The Realm standing in the doorway of her bathroom. "If you don't mind, Mr. Reynolds, I'd like to retch in private."

Mathis leans against the doorframe. "Felicity you've been in this state twice already this evening. Do you not remember?"

"I do not. I do, however, remember that my husband is dead, my children are gone, and you have entered my home uninvited."

"Felicity, have you forgotten who I am? Perhaps you've been rendered clueless by the bump to your head?"

"No, Mr. Reynolds, I am not clueless. I am fucking pissed."

"About?" he asks flatly.

Felicity scoffs. She runs her hand across her mouth and pulls herself to her feet. She leans over the sink, cups water in her hands, sucks it into her mouth and swishes it around. She cups some more and splashes the cold wetness against her face. She grabs her toothbrush and angrily attacks the bitter taste left from the day's events. When she finishes, she turns to the man who silently waits for his answer. "Mr. Reynolds, the items on the list of things that piss me off are too numerous to name, even if I were mentally able to do so."

"Pick one," he directs.

"I suppose I am most pissed by my hubris," she says as she pushes past.

He spins around and leans against the wall facing the master bedroom, "Yes. Hubris. It is a challenge to master and to judge, but I think in this case you are selling yourself short. I do not find excessive pride in you, Felicity, and your self-confidence is justified."

She stares blankly at him from the edge of the bed, presses her feet firmly on the floor in a feeble attempt to fight the spin of the room. She refuses to lie down for fear it will be analyzed as a sign of weakness. "This is not the kind of man to show one's underbelly," she whispers.

"See, no hubris."

Felicity fixes her stare and rides the waves of nausea until they subside, then offers her thoughts. "I believe the bile I just spewed held the last of my self-confidence, certainly the last of my dignity, Mr. Reynolds."

He shakes his head, "That was self-pity mixed with your bile. You know the difference. If for some reason your head injury caused confusion on this point, all you need do is look around at who **is** and who **is not** still on my team."

Mathis pushes off the doorjamb and walks past her. "Sleep it off, Felicity. I want you back in fighting form in the morning."

A Fred Serpico riff.

The RFI jet taxis at the Halifax airport readying to take Fred Serpico, Mike Monopoli, John Maxwell, and Shelby Webber back to the States. The breaking news about the death of Paul Ferraro, aka Boston, aka paid killer for The Realm, was broadcast shortly after midnight. RFI and FBI colleagues made a mad dash from The Compound and are nearly airborne. It's just after 3 AM, and their workday has begun.

"Okay," Fred unbuckles and takes a standing position in the middle aisle. "Same plan. RFI will focus on the Reynolds brothers and bringing Leavy home. The way I see it, John and Shelby need to do some serious defensive work. If we're right, The Realm is going to make a move to get the preeminent cyber defender. Right now, they have one cyber huntress, and we have two. We have a stronger offensive team, which means Joy and Annie can go where Leavy goes and thwart whatever she is forced to do. The best short-term plan for the nefarious ones is to get the preeminent defender to block Joy's and Annie's efforts. That's the surest way for The Realm to secure the upper hand. John, you've bought yourself some time with the lie you told about Stacy Remington's files and computers. The Realm went to great lengths to have that stuff torched. So long as they think you have that stockpile, they're gonna let you roam about, but if they start wondering whether you really have the stuff, Jack McGovern is gonna make a move to get you. I'm sure he'll have some interesting ways to make you talk, John, and we both know you won't like his methods."

Fred takes a few steps, turns around and retraces those steps, "Fuck, I need a window." His fellow passengers point to the little rectangular glass things running the length of the jet. "Those are not windows and the stuff outside them is passing at Mach speed."

John groans, "Fucking flying tin can."

Mike laughs.

John evil eyes him, "Something to say, Monopoli?"

"No, sir."

Fred stops the back and forth, "Okay, Director Webber, The Realm is going to take you out if you give them the chance. They no longer have an option. You know too much. You suspect Jack McGovern. You've aligned yourself with John Maxwell, who is aligned with RFI, and your second in command knows you and John were away for the holiday. He'll assume the two of you were together and maybe with RFI."

Shelby nods.

"You're gonna need protection on-site other than John. Who do you trust at the Bureau?"

"Agent Amanda Rhys."

"What's her story?"

"She's two years at the FBI. Her employment title is assistant to the director and deputy director. She's plugged into the day to day operations of the top floors."

"Two years in, why is she at a desk job?" Fred intrigues.

"Her first and last field assignment was the FBI/DEA sting in Sherman Oaks, California, where we lost two agents and several civilians. I brought her in from the field."

"Why?"

"Rhys was at the top of her graduating class at Quantico. She made quite the impression at the Academy. When the sting fell apart, her actions were deemed exemplary, and she was credited with service above and beyond, but I felt she needed time to process the events of that night and feared we might lose her if she didn't come in from the field. I plugged her in at the top of the Bureau to give her a breather and to show her I had confidence in her."

John adds in, "Rhys is the agent who got the hinky feeling when she saw Jack McGovern coming out of Shelby's office. She was about to contact the director after hours to report his breach of protocol."

Fred nods. "Okay, Director, you trust her, but is she ready to go undercover as your security detail? She'll be between a rock and a hard place, protecting one of her bosses from the other?"

John and Shelby answer in unison, "She's ready."

"Your call. Let's move on. Mike and I need to be seen while we're in DC. The Realm thinks RFI is going to review Stacy's files, so they'll expect us to be where the stuff is, and we need them to see us, at certain times. Our being local will accomplish a few things: 1) It brings credibility to John's lie about having Stacy's stuff on The Realm and Tango. 2) It will test and strain Jack McGovern's surveillance team. They aren't going to be able to attach ears to us, but they're gonna have to put eyes on us. For the first few days that extra workload will mean less visuals on John and Shelby. 3) Mike and I will provide John and Shelby's security until we can get Agent Rhys up to speed. Agreed?"

"Agreed."

"On a side note, Researcher Randy is going to focus his efforts on finding out the who and how of the prison poisonings. The commonality between the deaths of Dan Shea, Dominique Brettenvue, and Paul Ferraro, is that they were all poisoned behind prison walls. The anomaly is that they were in different prisons. This method of killing requires external work and internal work. External work, poisoning the food and making sure it gets to the correct prison; internal work, having Realm people on shift during food delivery, and prohibiting any intervention during the prisoners' last moments alive. These killings prove The Realm is plugged into the Federal prison system. That didn't happen overnight, it took coordination, probably years of groundwork. The Realm is in the phase of cutting loose ends. So far, the snipping hasn't included the ancillary leaders involved in Tango. I think we can agree that's a temporary situation. Antonio Alvarez, Binto Dube, Roland Gaffney, Castro López, Julio Romero, Raphael Ruiz, Stiles Sigüenza, and Migel Sosa are locked in solitary confinement cells across the country, but I'm sure they know there's an elimination list and they are on it. Roland Gaffney has to be sweating a bit. John, you might want to pay him a visit and start pushing a few of his buttons."

Shelby begins to speak.

John shakes his head and squeezes her hand.

Fred continues, "Again, John, this is for you and Director Webber. Let's assume Jack McGovern is on the leadership level of The Realm. If the Octopus organizational chart is correct, there is The Body and eight arms. If Mathis Reynolds is The Body and Eli Reynolds and Jack McGovern are arms, we have two of the eight appendages identified. We need more,

John. I think there's some diving in your future, targeted diving. We need to know everyone at leadership level and figure out the identity of the new assassin. I'm putting Penny Meehan on this. She's the one who linked the paratroopers call 'Geronimo' to the doctor, lawyer, Indian chief comment made by Celia Brettenvue, and she identified Boston as her would-be assassin. When Penny gave us that puzzle piece, it allowed us to connect Paul Ferraro to Mason Trellis and the two of them to The Realm. Penny is an Army reservist and is already familiar with the research Leavy did on the special forces. There is no stretch needed to think the new assassin is affiliated with the rangers. I want Penny on this piece of the investigation. She needs to take control. She needs to turn the tables and become the hunter after her three rounds of being the hunted."

There are nods all around.

Fred continues. "Deniability here, Director Webber?"

She nods.

"Joy is diving deep on Senator Turner Rodgers. If he's involved in this shit fest, he's gonna take a step away from The Realm to concentrate on the 2020 election. I don't peg Rodgers as an arm. I think he sits directly below Mathis, and if that's the case and he steps back for 2020, then there's gonna be a new person put into his position. The Realm has taken some pretty big hits and is at a weak point. Mathis and Eli have gone into hiding, Turner Rodgers is on his way out or will be scaling back, two assassins are dead, and investigations into the organization and its members are heating up. This is the time for an organizational shift, particularly at the top. Joy and Rocco are going to work this piece of the puzzle."

There is silence when Fred finishes. He stares at his colleagues, "Well?" he asks.

John smirks at the man, "You're finished?"

"Yeah, I'm finished," Fred chuckles.

"When you're done with one of your riffs, Fred, you need to let us know. Otherwise, you'll never hear any of us speak."

Control.

    Manuel Xavier wakes December 26th and takes control. His voice is raspy, his hands shake easily, and his eyes are quick to lose focus, but he takes control. "No more sedatives," he tells his doctor.

    "I welcome your input, Mr. Xavier, but I call the shots," Dr. Weinstock says with a ready smile.

    "Great, hospital humor," Manuel groans.

    "Ah, my son is back," Rocco beams as he enters the medical suite. "Doctor, your real work begins now. Manuel is an impatient man, a stubborn man, and I suspect a man who knows of the things we tried to keep from him."

    "Where is Leavy?"

    "We're working on it, son." Rocco's words do not please the patient. A cacophony of beeps and hisses alert those around him of his internal turmoil.

    "Mr. Xavier, calm down, or I will do it for you," the doctor warns.

    Manuel snarls dismissively, then looks beyond the doctor to his father.

    Rocco chuckles, "Manuel, Dr. Weinstock and his team are armed Federal agents. If they are inclined to sedate you, it is a fait accompli. I suggest you do what does not come easily for you: behave and follow directions. Si?"

He nods.

"Good." Rocco takes a seat. "I'll answer your questions and inform you of our plans to find Leavy and bring her home. You will receive the information calmly, or you will be sedated. Understood?"

He nods.

"Before we discuss Leavy, I have questions for you. Do you know who shot you?"

"Mathis Reynolds. Eli Reynolds took Leavy." There is no hesitation or hedging in his answer.

Rocco nods and works to tamp down his own internal turmoil and rage. His focus is swiftly returned to his son when Manuel becomes increasingly agitated and grabs hold of his father's arm.

"Eli desires Leavy. He won't kill her. He will rape her." Manuel places his trembling hand over his heart. "I know in here that she is alive. Papa, she will do whatever it takes to survive, but she won't want to survive if he..."

The dangerously agitated man is sedated.

275 Market Street
Penny Meehan wakes December 26th completely out of control and muttering, "Find a penny, find a penny, find a penny."

Ted grabs hold of her and pulls her into his spoon, "It was a nightmare. You're here with me. You're safe." Ted spins her beneath him, "Penny …"

"Don't. Call. Me. That." Her seething words fade into a torrent of tears.

"You were chanting, repeating the same thing over and over."

"What did I say?" she sniffles through racked breathing.

"Find a penny." Ted loses his woman into herself…

Penny took another quick look out Ted's window. "The Honda isn't parked where Kelly normally parks it." She eyed the woman walking to the front door. "That's not Kelly. Her walk is off. Her energy is off." She raced to the little area between Ted's office and the den, unlatched the top of a hidden door and snuck into the root cellar seconds before the doorbell rang and the front door opened. Penny didn't move from her perch on the top step.

The woman called out, "Hi Penny, it's Kelly." Silence. "Hey, Penny, did you forget about our session?" Silence.

Penny crouched as the assassin searched the first floor and ran to the second floor. She took that opportunity to move from the top step down into the root cellar. Doors slamming and furniture flipping covered the sounds of Penny's breathing and banging heart. She counted the footfalls as they made their way back to the first floor – held her breath when they stopped on the other side of the hidden door.

"Where the fuck are you?"

Penny mentally tracked the assassin's movements through the kitchen and out onto the breezeway. She wrapped herself tight to ward off the cold, stared at the stone-cold space heater, imagined it was throwing off heat. A shake took hold, fueled by the frigid temps and sheer terror of the assassin's song.

"Find a Penny, shoot the fuck, all day long, you'll have good luck."

Penny began whispering, "Ted, please come home. Ted, please come home. Ted. Come. Home."

The – penny – drops!

"Find a penny, shoot the fuck, all day long, you'll have good luck."

"Jesus, Lucky."

Chevy Chase, Maryland
Felicity Ferraro wakes December 26th and takes control. Her voice is raspy, her hands shake easily, and her eyes are quick to lose focus, but

she takes control. "You need to leave," she tells The Body upon entry to her kitchen.

"Still suffering from your concussion, I see," he says flatly.

"I am perfectly well. I think it's best that you go."

Mathis stands from his seat. "Come here, Felicity."

She hesitates, then crosses the room. Her spine is ramrod straight, though her legs barely hold, and her heart thunders deep. She stops and crosses her arms over her rapidly rising and falling chest.

Mathis closes the space between them and raises his hand to touch her cheek.

She flinches.

His eyes flash with anger, "I do not hit women."

"No, you kill them." She moves away.

His hand encircles her wrist. "I took no pleasure in killing my wife. Stacy is dead because she became my enemy."

Felicity lifts a haughty brow, "And my husband, did you take pleasure in killing him?"

"I took great pleasure in killing him because he became your enemy." Mathis runs his thumb across her lips, gazes long at budded nipples pressing against taut blue cotton, then steps back from his obvious want. "Let me know when you are ready for me." With that, Mathis Reynolds leaves the widow, making mental note that she has yet to shed a tear for her deceased husband.

Snowfall Prison

Hannah Leavy wakes December 26th completely out of control and muttering, "Whatever it takes. **Whatever** it takes. To survive." Her voice is raspy, her hands shake easily, and her eyes are quick to lose focus, but she takes control. She calls out to her captor, "I'm awake." She sits at the edge of the bed, waits for his approach, and hopes he stays back. She smiles when he remains at the doorjamb and tosses the key onto the bed. She takes the cold metal, bends over her knees, and pretends to unlock the chains she never attached the night before.

The rapist, who thinks of himself as Leavy's lover, was sloppy after he drugged and defiled her. He held her in his arms on the comfort couch near a lovely fire as though they were a satisfied couple. When he hungered, he prepared them a midnight snack, encouraged her to tell stories of her life, then waited for her to shower and dress for bed. He watched from the doorway as she moved her chains into place, but he never inspected the lock to make sure it was fastened. It was the first time he forgot to check—or maybe he knew she didn't chain herself. "Maybe last night was a test," she whispers.

Memories of his kisses and his hands touching her—his manhood filling her—is a test of another kind…

After dinner Eli took Leavy to the comfort room. "We are going to sit on the couch and talk. My gift to you is that I am not going to chain you. I slipped a mild relaxant into your dinner. It is strong enough to keep you from running, and it will help loosen you for things to come."

Her stomach churned. Her silent mantra began. *An FBI agent does **whatever** it takes to survive.*

Eli pulled her onto his lap. She felt the hardness of his desire pulse beneath her. She tried to push away. Her mind was a mess, her body no longer her own. *Whatever it takes.*

"Lift your dress and remove your panties," he directed. She was slow to move. "Leavy, don't ruin this evening," he warned.

She lifted her dress to her hips, he pulled it over her head. When she returned to his lap, he slid in. There was no resistance. He filled her, kissed her, touched her, released her. She hated her body for betraying her, for betraying Manuel.

Once safely behind closed bathroom doors, the broken woman washed away her pain and shame, then the former FBI agent made a

plan. "Gain his trust. Take small chances. Endure his sexual debasement. Wait for an opportunity. Fight until the bitter end. If you survive, return to Manuel. You have a plan, Agent Leavy. Stick to it."

*An assignment for you,
and you, and you.*

Fred and Mike checked into a hotel close to J. Edgar as soon as they arrived in DC. Before separating from John and Shelby, Fred went over the basics of their plan of action.

"Part A and B: offer protection to Director Webber and pull Agent Amanda Rhys in for security consultation and training, that's Mike's role. Part C and D: make a good showing so Jack McGovern's surveillance team knows where we are, then fuck with them, that's my role," Fred laughs big.

The RFI men are up and ready to move first thing. "Okay, Mike. Director Webber just confirmed she's working inside the FBI building all day. She'll be one on one with her assistant, Agent Rhys, and will update her through handwritten notes, then grab a conference room for a private conversation. She'll keep Rhys close throughout the day. When it's time for her to move from J. Edgar to her home, we'll make a transport plan. John will spend the day converting the director's home office into a diving center."

"Got it. Before I hook up with Webber and Rhys, I want to check out the security breach at Webber's waterfront home. If John found it, there's nothing to say other's haven't. Call me if you need me."

Fred begins his work with a call to Researcher Randy.

"Yo."

"Yo, yourself."

"Speak to me, Detecting One," Randy laughs.

Fred growls, "Listen Kid, I'm putting you on the who and how of the prison poisonings. Dan Shea, Dominique Brettenvue, and Paul Ferraro were poisoned in three different prisons. It's highly unlikely that one person handled all three killings inside the walls, so we're looking at three different inside players. Do a deep dive on employees at each of the detention centers. See if there's a 'now you see me, now you don't' employee, maybe someone new to the facility just before the killings or an established someone who left on vacation and never came back."

"On it, Fred."

"Before you go, have you seen Ted or Penny today?"

"I've seen Ted and he's out for blood, the kind that flows from assassins," Randy says before disconnecting.

Detective Serpico calls Detective Brothers. "Theodore, do I have to come to Lewisburg to settle you?"

"No, but if you show up, I'm in Hufnagle working through some rage, so don't fuck with me."

"Did Penny cut through some shit?"

"Fuck, Fred. You know that children's ditty, find a penny—"

"—pick it up, all day long, you'll have good luck," Fred finishes.

"Yeah, except in this case it's, 'find a penny, shoot the fuck, all day long, you'll have good luck,'" Ted growls. "The assassin chanted that shit over and over as she tore my house apart looking for my woman. And Penny's been running parts of it through her head when she sleeps. The whole chant broke through this morning."

Fred runs that shit through his head, "Damn, Ted. Is Penny still together?"

"Yeah, she had a good cry, then she got out of bed and declared the assassin is ex-military. Penny started pacing the room and telling me what happened when she was holed up in the root cellar. It was like she was watching the shit show on some loop inside her head. After running it through, she said the assassin vowed to return and make Penny suffer for fucking up her mission. That memory screwed Penny's head back on straight. She's pissed as fuck, Fred. She's upstairs in the apartment speed keyboarding looking for something on the internet that might identify the assassin."

There's a noticeable exhale on Fred's end. "Theodore, I said it before, but it deserves repeating, I'm crushing on your woman."

"Too late, Fred, Lucky already consented to go on a honeymoon with me. All we need to do before we set a wedding date is shut down a crime syndicate called The Realm, which is run by a man named The Body, who thinks of himself as the centralized part of an Octopus, and has severed one set of leadership arms, which have since regenerated. Shit, Fred, the only way I'll ever park my ass on a sandy beach with my wife is if The Body ends up dead."

"I'm good with that, Theodore."

When Penny answers her phone, she is singing along with the ringtone, "…Ooo, ooo, ooo, I feel Luckyyyyy."

Fred laughs heartily. "I just told your man that I have a crush on you, your off-key singing isn't gonna change that fact."

"Fred Serpico, how the hell are you?" Penny chirps.

"I'm smiling wide, Ms. Meehan. I think you'll be smiling wide in a minute. I want to turn a piece of the investigation over to you. Do you have thoughts on this particular subject?"

"If it's hunting the assassin I'm all-in, Serpico."

"Well, then, I guess you're all-in, Meehan. Have Randy give you a set of printouts of the work Leavy did when we were looking for Boston. Fresh eyes this time. Don't only look for the woman assassin, look for others who might be involved in aiding and abetting her. If we can isolate potential Realm resources and get eyes on them, it might lead us to the bigger targets in our investigation."

"Fred, I was thinking, the first woman to finish Army ranger training graduated in 2018, and she's still active duty. That means our assassin isn't a ranger, she's most likely a trained sniper who worked with special forces, maybe trained with them or provided training to them. If so, she's been accepted by the elite military division in recognition of her skill set. Although military women weren't always welcome on the front lines, their skills were identified and used behind the scenes and rewarded with honorary titles. I'll be focusing my research on the stuff Leavy has on snipers and survivalists. That's where I'm gonna find my would-be assassin."

"Hey, Penny, tell Ted I'm no longer crushing on you. I'm head over heels."

Penny hangs up with a song in her heart and tripping from her lips, "...Ooo ooo ooo, I feel Luckyyyyy ..."

Powerful men.
Brilliant women.

Rocco and Joy have been locked in the Computer Center since before dawn. Copious coffee consumption and intense concentration has been the order of things, so the mid-morning knock at the door is met with an enthusiastic welcome for the food-bearing Annie.

"I figure you two are here for the duration, but you still need to eat." She hands each a warming sack with homemade sandwich rolls stuffed full with ham and cheese omelets. Then she hands off cooling sacks with bowls of fruit salad and bottled water. Set on top is a napkin fully adorned with tiny lipstick kisses. Annie rolls her eyes as she explains. "The mothers are having a makeup party with the kids at the Main Cottage. You are now in possession of irrefutable evidence of the lipstick assault. I saved a kiss-napkin for Fred and cannot wait for the ensuing conversation he has with my mom about including Joseph in beauty makeovers. There's video evidence as well, but I'm saving that for a private screening with the Detecting One."

Rocco and Joy enjoy Annie's devilish plan.

She points to a kiss inside a red heart, "That's Charlotte's. I made a kiss-napkin for Manuel for when he's feeling better."

Rocco pulls Annie in for a long hug and a loving kiss to the top of her head. "Grazie, Piccolo One."

Annie steps onto the feet of the former U.K. cyber intelligence officer and current leader of the internationally acclaimed crime-busting organization RFI. She raises a finger, pulls a tube of lipstick from her pocket, applies a healthy swipe, wraps her arms around his neck, and places a loud smack on his cheek. "There, you've been lipstick assaulted." She steps off his feet and orders him to, "Eat that food. I'll be back with lunch. Today's offering is Chicken Caesar Salad with a side of bread and wine. I'm calling it, Kitt Mahoney's Last Supper. Bye."

Joy takes a bite of sandwich, then heads to one of the whiteboards. She thinks a bit, then draws an octopus. She begins labeling and narrating.

"<u>Mathis Reynolds</u>. There is enough evidence to designate him as The Body of The Realm. He has been identified as the shooter of Manuel Xavier, and his whereabouts are currently unknown." She labels the body of the octopus with that information.

"<u>Eli Reynolds</u>. There is enough evidence to designate him an ancillary leader of The

Realm. He has been identified as the kidnapper of Hannah Leavy, and his whereabouts are currently unknown. She labels an arm of the octopus with that information.

"Jack McGovern. There is enough evidence to designate him an ancillary leader of The Realm. His proximity to Remington and Webber provided ample opportunity for snooping, and his whereabouts are being monitored." She labels an arm of the octopus with that information.

Rocco remains silent during the whiteboarding. He knows this isn't an organizational exercise for Joy; she is deep in processing mode and will have a diving strategy figured out when she is finished.

"Fred and John will be doing a full 360 on the above-named individuals, so they are off our plate. I expect that should help tamp your lust for revenge against the Reynolds brothers, Mr. Fiancetti?"

"Temporarily, Mrs. Fiancetti."

She smiles wide, "Understood." She touches his cheek as she passes to a second whiteboard. She titles the top, Turner Rodgers. "The RFI cyber team is going to focus on this man." She begins labeling and narrating. "Senator Rodgers is the presumptive GOP presidential candidate in the 2020 election. We have a lot to discuss here, but I'll come back to him later."

She draws a line halfway down the whiteboard and labels the lower section, <u>Paul Ferraro, aka Boston</u>. "The recently murdered Mr. Ferraro was a contract assassin of The Realm."

"Payback's a bitch."

Joy's giggle is accompanied with a raised eyebrow, "A fourth dialect? I'm very used to the upper crust of your British-speak, and the suave of your Italian-growl, and the absurdity of your Rocco-kitsch, but I am unfamiliar with American-slang."

"Woman, I am multi-lingual."

Joy howls in laughter, "Woman? Did you just call me, Woman?"

"Yeah."

"Oh. My. God. Stop with the American. Please."

He smiles wide, "Si, but I will not abandon my other tongues."

"I'm counting on it," she laughs big.

He winks, "Perhaps I will recite Machado's poetry in his native Spanish, or serenade a Persian love song in Farsi, or…"

"Yes, Yes! Use your tongue any way you want," she winks, "but do it later. We have work to do."

"Pushy broad."

Joy laughs heartedly, "Enough, please. Here's the story of Paul Ferraro. He killed Abigail Forrester, a known irritant and probable blackmailer of Turner Rodgers. He killed Celia Brettenvue, an FBI informant who'd been telling tales about a Realm project known as Tango. As for the killing of Dominique Brettenvue, Ferraro most likely had a hand in her murder. She languished in prison a good stretch of time before she met her maker. Two circumstances could have attributed to her death—she's the daughter of Celia and Benton Brettenvue, both of whom had associations with Realm members, one of whom was telling tales, and Dominique was spilling family secrets of her own to her attorney, Granger Mitchell. Legal discussions don't usually warrant a death-sentence, but Dominique knew an awful lot about The Realm, and Granger is an associate of Fred Serpico. Someone inside Lewisburg Penitentiary probably heard enough from Dominique's and Granger's meetings to report back that she was a traitor to the organization. The Body doesn't hesitate when dealing with traitors. And then there's the assassination of FICA Director, Stacy Remington. She was the 'big kill' of Paul Ferraro. Through her position at the FBI, Stacy Remington unwittingly provided Mathis Reynolds with his power base—"

"Intelligence."

"Yes. The husband had his wife under surveillance at J. Edgar and at her home office. For more than a decade, Mathis Reynolds, aka The Body, got what he needed from the FICA director. The reason Stacy is dead is not because she outlived her usefulness, but because she continued an unsanctioned, secretive investigation. The director was cutting too close to the bone. When push came to shove, the husband neutralized the wife, severing his information stream to save his organization."

Joy pauses and ponders before continuing. "As for Penny Meehan, the lone survivor of Paul Ferraro's elimination project. She's an investigative reporter who may have found something about the presidential candidate or about the organization during a digging expedition in DC. We need to interview Penny to see what she remembers and what she has in her files."

"Si."

Joy moves to a third whiteboard and titles the top, Replacement. She steps back and reviews her work. "Rocco, let's assume Turner Rodgers has been part of The Realm from Day One. Let's also assume that he isn't a leader arm. If The Realm wants him in the Oval Office, they can't risk exposing him as a dangling appendage, so his role may have been nothing more than a conduit between The Body and The Arms. With Eli in a leadership position, Mathis had eyes on the ancillary leaders and on Turner. The brothers could compare directives with deliverables and keep everyone in line. Now that

Eli is in hiding with Leavy, Mathis doesn't have that level of control. He won't know if Turner is following his instructions to the letter. He's going to need someone he trusts as his new conduit."

Rocco interrupts his wife, "He'll choose a woman for that role. He hasn't had success with the men in his organization: Roland Gaffney, Paul Ferraro, Mason Trellis, or the eight men associated with Tango; they're all dead or imprisoned. Dominique Brettenvue was the highest ranking woman in his organization and Stacy Remington was the most plugged in woman at the FBI. They were very useful to Mathis Reynolds."

"Yes, and they're dead. On that point, The Body has a penchant for killing women. In short order he had Abigail, Celia, Dominique, and Stacy killed, and minus an incredible run of luck, Penny would also be dead. I'm convinced Mathis Reynolds will replace Turner Rodgers with a woman, and empirical evidence suggests she may have a short lifespan." Joy thinks for a few minutes before adding on, "Men at that level of power typically surround themselves with brilliant women—they feed off them, sexually and intellectually."

Rocco makes a move on his wife, walks her backward until she is pressed tight against a wall. "Don't I know it, Woman" the growl settling in his throat is quickly replaced with a groan at the interruption of his ringing cell. He pulls away when he reads the caller ID. "It's Mick Bentley."

Joy pecks her husband's cheek, "Take it, but be prepared to finish this later."

"Si." He adjusts his bulge, "Not much later I hope."

"Ready when you are," she winks.

Lecturing the beast.

Mick Bentley, Inspector General of the United Kingdom Secret Intelligence Service, and best friend of Rocco Fiancetti, gets right to the crux, "Are you secure, Rocco?"

"Si."

"You did not call me after Manuel's death."

"Si."

"You did not call Maverick Cross after Manuel's death."

"Si."

"For the same reason."

"Si."

Mick exhales the breath he's held since hearing the news report of Manuel's killing. "I've been in communication with Maverick in compliance with our plan. Since neither of us heard from you, we were 99% sure that Manuel was still alive. How is he?"

"Awake, ornery, and fighting back. His physical injuries are healing well. His emotional injuries, not so much."

Mick pulls a deep breath, "Leavy?"

"Si."

"She was taken?"

Rocco chokes his confirmation, "Si, The Realm has #3."

Mick gives his friend a moment, then pushes in. "Rocco, I fear RFI made a tactical mistake by not reaching out to agencies and asking for help the minute she was taken. I know why you wanted to keep it quiet, but your silence is working against you. Deep chatter is beginning that Leavy is no longer under the protection of RFI. Speculation is ramping up that she is in the hands of the nefarious ones. The Realm isn't the only faction who would like a huntress of her caliber in their ranks. If there's speculation that she is vulnerable, then there are plans to find her and take her."

"How pervasive is the chatter?"

"Limited to certain groups, but when it bubbles to the surface, which it will, the world will know that the third-ranked cyber huntress is vulnerable. That will make her fair game and will put a very high price on her head."

There is a long silence between the men.

Mick breaks it, "Rocco, I fear the beast of vengeance is with you again, and you are contemplating action. If you surrender to temptation you may not walk away as freely as you did when you avenged Eleni. Your son lives, Rocco. Let that satisfy the beast."

Change is good.

Ted Brothers sits in a conference room at the police station he has called home for the past twelve years. His commanding officer, Nathan Cruise, and two Internal Affairs investigators have called him in for a little chit-chat about the murdered physical therapist, Kelly Thompson. The Philly detective told no one at 275 where he was headed; he validates that decision. "Don't want or need anyone's input. Today is about change," he reminds himself—he prepares himself. A restlessness rises in the man. Ted gets up and paces a bit, answers the demand for something to distract him, a tactile relief; he pensively moves his thumb to touch a wedding ring that no longer claims his finger. He shakes his head, reaches into his pocket, pulls a penny and begins moving it between his thumb and his forefinger. "Change has already come," he smiles.

After being kept waiting for nearly an hour, the inquisitors enter. Ted quickly reflects on the time he's spent with these men—the gritting through cases, the reveling in one another's personal joys, the shouldering of one another's personal grief. In this room, at this moment, they are not standing shoulder to shoulder. **They** are a team, and he is on his own.

After five minutes of silence, his CO begins, "Kelly Thompson, do you know her?"

"Not personally."

"Explain how you know her."

"I know of her in a professional capacity. She was the physical therapist treating the woman who's been staying with me."

"Penny Meehan."

"Yes."

The CO gets to the point of this little tête-à-tête. "Penny Meehan had a physical therapy session scheduled with Kelly Thompson on the morning of the young woman's murder. Is that correct?"

"Yes."

"Did that session take place?"

"No."

"Why is that?"

"The session did not take place because the therapist never showed for the appointment."

"Did Ms. Meehan call to find out why the therapist didn't show?"

"No."

"Why not?"

"We were getting ready for a trip out of town for the holidays. The time just got away from us. We figured Penny would call to reschedule the appointment when we came back from our trip."

"And are you back from your trip?" Cruise asks tersely.

"No. I'm back for this conversation. And I'm about done here." Ted gets up to leave.

His commanding officer tells him to sit, "Internal Affairs wants a chance to pick at the rest of your bones, Brothers."

"Bet they do." He remains standing.

"Detective, tell us what you know about Mason Trellis, the man you killed."

Ted reaches into his pocket, pulls his badge and places it on the conference room table, "Gentlemen, I no longer work for the Philadelphia Police Department. Unless you are placing me under arrest, I am leaving. If you want to discuss this matter further, contact my attorney to set an appointment." Ted fingers through several cards in his wallet and places one onto the table; it's the one Granger Mitchell handed him the day they first met.

The Commanding Officer reads it then passes it to the Internal Affairs guys.

Ted hears one of the men say, "We're fucked," as the door closes behind former Philly Detective Theodore Brothers.

Ted swings by his house, grabs a few things and is on his way back to 275 by late afternoon. On his way, he calls Granger and gives a brief synopsis. He exhales fully when Granger suggests the former detective stop by his apartment when he gets back to Lewisburg. Brothers no sooner ends that call when an unidentified number appears on his cell. He lets it go to voicemail then immediately listens to it.

Detective Brothers, this is Officer Os Landry. I wanted to talk to you before you left the station, but it didn't seem like the right time. If you could call me, it's important. Maybe.

Ted returns the young officer's call, "What's up, Os?"

"Two things, sir. On a few occasions, over the course of a couple days, I intersected with a cherry red Camaro on your street. At first I thought someone new moved into the neighborhood and had a sweet ride. Now, I think it was casing your house."

"Who was driving the Camaro?"

"A female, sir. I had a hinky feeling, so I pulled up stolen vehicle records and there is a report about a boosted Camaro from a neighborhood not too far from Granger Mitchell's place."

"A sweet, cherry red one?"

"Yes, sir."

"When was it boosted?"

"November 5th. The day of the Lewisburg mayoral election and—"

"—the day Celia Brettenvue was murdered at the Mitchell estate," Ted finishes.

"Yes, sir, that's right."

"What's the second thing, Landry?"

"A torched vehicle with a body inside was found by a couple kids in Beaver Falls, Pennsylvania. The car and the body are staying put until spring. I've got a hinky feeling about this, too, sir."

"Good work. Officer Landry, you ought to put everything you've got into your career. You have what it takes, Os."

Ted can feel the smile and puffed up pride of the officer through the phone.

"If I have anything else to share, should I contact you, sir?"

"I'm bad news right now. I'm gonna text you a number. It's for RFI Detective Fred Serpico, you met him at my place. Do not share that number with anyone, but use it if you get another hinky feeling. He'll get the information to me. And contact him if you ever need anything."

"Yes, sir. Good luck, sir."

"Be safe out there, Landry."

275

Granger Mitchell is waiting for Ted Brothers to arrive. He's set a legal pad and pen at the kitchen table and had Randy set a tripod camera for a contemporaneous recording of the day's events.

Faye answers Ted's knock and leads him to Granger. The detective smiles when he sees the setup, "No wonder the guys back at the station started sweating when I left your business card. By the way, I need another one, Granger."

"I'll give you a handful, Ted."

Shadow figure.

Fred receives three picture texts. They are of the whiteboards at the Computer Center that Joy uses to lay out a case. The first text is of a hand-drawn octopus, the body labeled, Mathis Reynolds. Fred starts reading. He stops at the words: **Mr. Reynolds has been identified as the shooter of Manuel Xavier.** He's on his feet pacing when he calls Joy, "What the fuck?"

"That was fast, Fred," Joy laughs. "Lots of stuff has happened since you left The Compound."

Fred checks his watch, "I left fifteen hours ago Joy."

"Yeah, well, your son wears lipstick. Manuel identified his shooter as Mathis Reynolds, and he confirmed it was Eli Reynolds who took Leavy. I doubt you read that far before you called me," again, she laughs.

"Joy, tell me Rocco hasn't gone after Mathis. I've got enough shit on my plate. I don't need to be traipsing all over hell and creation trying to find him before he finds Manuel's shooter."

"He's here. He needs to talk to you, but my stuff needs to go first. Don't interrupt me, Fred."

The detective laughs big at the tables being turned, "Wouldn't think of it, Joy."

"Take a minute and familiarize yourself with the whiteboards. Let me know when you're done, or we can take them piece by piece if you want."

"Piece by piece. I want to spend a minute on the titles you have on the octopus and add this: Under Eli Reynolds put *sniper division,* and under Jack McGovern put *surveillance division.* I think as we move through, we should try to identify the other arms by thinking about job titles. Legitimate organizations need a financial handler, a damage control handler, a personnel handler, etc. This organization needs snipers, surveillance, and whatever else one would need for world domination."

"Yes. That's good, Fred."

"John and Shelby are working on identifying the eight arms, but I think you should join in with them. Create a criminal organizational flowchart and work it from that end. The leaders are probably all in the DC power structure, so Shelby will have some unique insights into this."

"On it."

"Before you go, Joy, I left the Turner Rodgers files at The Compound, so—"

"Sorry for the interruption and a swerve to the right, Fred, but someone needs to talk to Penny Meehan to see if she found something incriminating on Rodgers when she was in DC snooping around. She didn't keep her trip to the

Nation's capital a secret and was pretty deep in the weeds on the senator and his purported campaign manager, so Penny definitely got the attention of certain people, the ones who would know if she were inching toward pay dirt. I think Penny knows something, even if she doesn't realize it, and that's why The Realm keeps taking whacks at her."

Before Joy lets Fred disconnect, she throws all-in. "Now, about the assignment you gave me. You wanted me to find out who is going to replace Turner Rodgers. I don't have any concretes, but I have a lot of thoughts, so you should run what I say as things I think, rather than things I can prove."

"Yeah. Go ahead."

"Turner Rodgers has been part of The Realm since Day One. He's not a leader arm because the organization can't risk losing him. He's their long game, the person they want in the Oval Office. Instead of Turner being a dangling arm, I think he is Mathis Reynolds' messenger, a conduit between The Body and The Arms."

"Hold up Joy, something's nagging me. I need to process ……. okay, I've got a thread. What if The Arms think Turner Rodgers is The Body, that he is head honcho of The Realm and they have pledged allegiance to him. Give me another minute, Joy." He takes many. "We've been operating under the assumption that the ancillary leaders don't know about Leavy's kidnapping—maybe they don't even know Mathis Reynolds is The Body. I need another minute." He takes many. "If Mathis Reynolds is at the top of this organization and the only people who know that fact are Eli and Turner, and Mathis thinks his back is against the wall, he might disband The Realm. Think about it. All he'd have to do is kill Turner Rodgers. With that one move, the organization is finished, the ancillary leaders walk away thinking their leader is dead, and Mathis Reynolds walks away without anyone knowing he was the person in power."

"**We know** he's The Body, Fred."

"Yeah. Let's look at that. The Reynolds brothers are already in the wind. The ancillary leaders of The Realm can't give us shit about Mathis Reynolds because they think Turner Rodgers is The Body. Turner can't give us shit because in this scenario he's dead. The imprisoned members of The Realm won't give us shit out of fear or hope that Mathis Reynolds will come around again. The FBI will be hamstrung and unable to go public with this, and Shelby Webber probably won't keep her job. Mathis Reynolds played this brilliantly—he's a shadow figure of a worldwide crime syndicate who can and will eliminate anyone who might be able to tie him to The Realm. I think this scenario is his end game and he'll fold his hand when he thinks we've gotten too close to him."

There is a measurable silence between the two before Joy adds to the fun and games. "There's more on this end."

Fred laughs, "Damn glad you're on our side!"

"If Turner is the messenger between The Body and The Arms, Mathis needs Eli in place to ensure that Turner holds to the letter of Mathis' directives. With Eli out of the picture, Mathis is vulnerable to a coup from within. Turner Rodgers has to step away from the organization during his 2020 campaign, so Mathis needs a replacement, someone he can trust."

"It'll be a woman," Fred tosses.

"That's what Rocco and I think."

"Hey, Joy, do me a favor, tell Rocco he's got himself a brilliant woman."

"He knows, Fred, he knows. I'm going to end this and go diving for a brilliant woman who might be working with Mathis Reynolds. Keep in touch."

Before Fred lets Joy disconnect, he asks another very important question, "Joy, did you say my son wears lipstick?"

She ends things on a huge laugh.

Don't whine about beer.

Shelby Webber spends the day at J. Edgar behind closed office doors. The only person with whom she interacts is Agent Amanda Rhys. Their verbal communication is economical, enhanced only by two handwritten notes from Shelby. The first lets the agent know the director's office and her briefcases are bugged. The second lets the agent know Shelby is going to ask her for a ride home and that the bugged briefcases are going along for the ride. Very little is said on the trip to Alexandria and what is said is limited to the weather and the holiday season.

John watches from inside Shelby's Potomac waterfront home for them to arrive. He is in the kitchen closing the oven door when they get upstairs.

"Good evening, Director Maxwell. Agent Rhys and I will be playing catch up from missed time over the holidays."

"Very well, Director."

"We will be in my office. What are your plans?"

"I have some analysis work upstairs and then dinner."

"Whatever is in that oven will be shared, Director Maxwell."

"Yes, Director Webber."

Shelby leads the way for the young agent who doesn't seem the least bit fazed by whatever it is that's transpiring.

The director of the FBI, the director of FICA, and Agent Rhys join Mike Monopoli, who has been waiting in Shelby's home office.

"Take a seat, Agent Rhys," the director directs. "I didn't bring you here to talk about the work you normally do at the Bureau. Agent, you are now on my security detail. Your thoughts on this?"

"Continue, ma'am."

"Very well. This is Mike Monopoli, reconnaissance and security specialist with Rocco Fiancetti Incorporated. He will be getting you up to speed on protective measures. Mike, the floor is yours."

"Agent Rhys, the first thing you need to know is that Deputy Director Jack McGovern is responsible for the bugging of the following people and locations: the J. Edgar offices of Director Webber and Director Maxwell, two briefcases Director Webber uses, the hotel room of Director Maxwell, and the office and home of former FICA Director Stacy Remington. In addition, the vehicles of all named parties have GPS tracking on them."

Agent Rhys nods as though she has figured all this out already.

Mike returns her nod. "I suspect your workstation at J. Edgar and your condo at Dupont Circle are currently being bugged by Jack McGovern's team. As soon as you arrive home this evening, your vehicle will be GPS trapped. Agent, are you still interested in this assignment?"

"Continue, Specialist Monopoli."

John and Shelby go downstairs for dinner while Rhys is supposedly upstairs working in Shelby's home office—she is actually in the lower level gym working with Mike. For the next many minutes, John's faux attempts to engage in work-related conversations are rebuffed by Shelby's faux headache. "I need a few minutes, Director Maxwell. I require food and drink in the most urgent way."

"Very well, Director. The food of the evening is Shepherd's Pie, and the drink is—"

"Wine." Shelby interrupts.

"No, ma'am. I am aware that you fancy yourself a wine connoisseur, but this hearty meal requires a pale lager." John ignores Shelby's groan and hands her a just-opened bottle of Molson Canadian. "No drinking glass required. Take it straight from the bottle, Director."

He waits.

She sips.

He begins. "Pale lagers are the most common beers, but they are very different from one another as are white wines."

Shelby groans again.

John ignores again. "Pale lagers are light gold in color, generally mild tasting, and always served cold. The conditioning and storage of lager beers begins with a cool, bottom-fermenting yeast process followed by maturation in cold storage. There is evidence that cold storage processing dates back to cave dwellers."

Shelby raises her bottle, "Perhaps we should toast cave dwellers past and present."

John laughs as he places a plate of Shepherd's Pie and a warm buttered roll in front of the beer snob.

Shelby inhales the warm steam rising from her plate and moans a little.

John remembers that moan, responds to that moan, then works to forget it when he remembers Jack McGovern's surveillance team is listening in. The beer enthusiast continues his lecture. "Pale lagers have a well-attenuated body and noble hop bitterness. That basically means the hops used for pale lagers are low in bitter and high in aroma. Pay attention, Director, you will find this next part interesting."

"Doubtful," she says around a mouthful of food.

"Oh, but you will. The low bitterness and strong aromas are attributes of European hops. As with grapes used in wines, the characteristics of hops is intricately tied to where they are grown. As for noble hops, they receive the official designation only if they are grown in areas deemed noble. Then the hops are given a noble name, Hallertau, Zatec, Spalt, and Tettnang."

Shelby leans back and folds her arms, "Mildly interesting, I suppose."

John smirks, "There's more."

"Yay," she offers with the roll of an eye.

He ignores her sarcasm, "Tisanes—you know, the herbal teas you are so fond of—they use hops and I'd be willing to bet that your favorite herbal teas use only noble hops."

Shelby leans back toward her dinnerplate, "Director Maxwell, I seem to have finished my beer. Please hand me another Molson and refrain from any further lectures."

John's smirk morphs into a smile—a great smile, "On it, ma'am."

Doggie bags and thoroughbred horses.

After a vending machine dinner of stale peanut butter crackers, a bag of candies that melt in your mouth *and* in your hand, and a sack of salt and vinegar chips, Fred calls his boss, and is greeted in typical Rocco-speak.

"Ah, Detecting One, my Only One said you'd be calling. You and Gia had quite the breakthrough on the organizational structure of The Realm, Confidences are such that we will find Mathis Reynolds and act accordingly."

"I trust there will be no action until we bring Leavy home, sir?"

"You have my word that my immediate focus stays on Leavy and The Realm. My revenge will wait, this cannot. I spoke with Mick Bentley at SIS. As you know, Mick is my former boss and a friend to me since the day Manuel was born. Years ago, I instructed Mick and another friend, Maverick Cross, that unless they heard directly from a Fiancetti that a Fiancetti was dead, then reporting of such event was false. Since no communique came from this end, they knew my son was alive. Mick relaxed with that knowledge, but took to the depths of cyberland when he began a concern about Leavy. He has found inceptions of chatter that our #3 is no longer under the protection of RFI and is suspected to be in the hands of the nefarious ones."

"Shit."

"Si. Mick suggests RFI made a tactical mistake by not asking agencies for help in looking for Leavy when she first disappeared. He understands our rationale, but I concede his point that we have opened Leavy to more troubles."

"Shit."

"Si. Mick's best cyber duo, Andria Covington and Vic Evans, are working this exclusively. Ms. Covington's current assessment is that the chatter is limited to certain groups and is still speculative. Once it is confirmed that Leavy is not in our hands, the cyber huntress will be considered fair game and will have a very high price on her head."

"Rocco, when I hang up from you, I'm gonna finish up a few things, then head back to 275 to work exclusively on getting Leavy back. You, Joy, John, and Shelby need to drill down on identifying The Arms and find out who replaced Turner Rodgers as The Body's go-to person. Finding that person is the best way to find Mathis Reynolds. Also, tell John to hold off on visiting Roland Gaffney at the Federal penitentiary. I'm having a nudge on that—it might mean there's a more effective string to pull. Let me find it and pull it before we put John in the same room with Gaffney. One upside right now is that Mike will stay in DC and have eyes on Jack McGovern while also providing security to Shelby and John."

Fred is interrupted by Mike entering the hotel room. "Hey, Rocco, Mike just got back. I'm gonna fill him in on Manuel identifying his shooter and the new plans. I'll check-in tomorrow." Fred disconnects and zooms in on a bag Mike placed on the hotel room table. "Is that food?"

"Yeah, John made Shelby dinner. He sent a doggie bag home for us."

Fred offers a skeptical look, "John cooks? Furthermore, John shares? He must be in the impress-the-woman phase of courtship. No complaints from this end so long as we are the beneficiaries of his attempt to woo the woman."

Mike laughs, "From what I've seen, he's already wooed that woman."

Mike eats while Fred fills him in.

Fred eats while Mike shares his plans.

"I'm gonna do a little more reconnaissance work then check-in with Agent Rhys before heading back to Webber's. I spent several hours with her. She's every bit as good as the director said. She's quick to put shit together and offers opinion and assessment. From that end, she's definitely ready for this assignment."

"I'm sensing a 'but' coming."

"She might be a bit too eager … might need some reigning in. When we were sparring in Director Webber's athletic room, I kept getting the image of a gated thoroughbred banging the post just before a run."

"Pretty descriptive Mike."

"Yeah, well, that's her vibe."

Dupont Circle

Amanda Rhys moves through her tiny studio apartment shedding one piece of clothing after another. She steps into a barely-big-enough-for-one-person shower, lathers with bodywash, and rinses with a blast of cold water. She is dried and zipping a pair of boyfriend jeans when Mike's words bang…

"I suspect your workstation at J. Edgar and your residence are currently being bugged by Jack McGovern's team. As soon as you arrive home this evening, your vehicle will be GPS trapped."

"Wish I remembered that **before** I traipsed around my place naked." She heads back to the bathroom, pulls her shoulder-length, dirty blonde hair into a high ponytail, and brushes her perfectly-straight teeth through two hummed choruses of the *Jeopardy!* theme song. As she heads back through her space, she shoves her feet into a pair of shitkickers, grabs her jacket, a wool watchman's cap, fingerless gloves, and her weapon. She checks her watch, "Ten minutes start to finish." She stands at the outside exit a long minute before moving. "Street clear. Still ten minutes was enough time to GPS my ride." She pushes back against the doorway when a car inches down the street sans headlights. When the ride slows in front of her brownstone, she key fobs her car's locks and watches the vehicle move quickly away. She is down the stairs, in her Jeep, and off her street within seconds.

"Where'd you go, Jack?"

Do bears shit in the woods?
Do agents?

Mike is confident Amanda can protect herself, though his confidence wanes with each passing minute and each unanswered call. After his fifth attempt to reach her fails, he leaves a friendly message, "Hey, Mandy. I'm in town for the night. I'd **really** like to see you. Give me a call." He bangs his hands on the steering wheel when he disconnects. "I should have put a fucking GPS on her ride before she left Webber's."

Alexandria Adjacent
Agent Rhys has been following Deputy Director McGovern for nearly twenty minutes, though they've only traveled about ten miles. Having spent the early part of the evening at Director Webber's waterfront home, she knows where she is. Sort of. "I should turn around and go home. I should call Mike Monopoli. He'll be pissed I'm out here, but maybe if I … What the eff? Where is Jack going?" The agent turns off her headlights before turning onto a dark cutaway road. She stops her vehicle, watches Jack's car continue a ways, stop in the middle of the street, then back up. "What's he…" She waits until the Escalade is deep into the trees and its lights darken before inching down the road and driving past. She goes a good ways

up the pitch-as-black road, finds a small path, and backs her Jeep in deep. She puts her hand in front of her face, "Nope." She twists in her seat and finds lights way off in the distance, "Webber's house?"

Within minutes, she is bitter cold and freaked the fuck out. "What the fuck am I doing?" She grabs her phone off the passenger seat, "Five missed calls. Good. Mike knows I'm missing." She climbs onto the passenger seat then down onto the well of the floor before returning his call.

A surge of relief floods Mike when he gets the call. That relief is short lived.

"Monopoli, I made a huge mistake and I'm in deep shit." Rhys whispers.

"Where are you?"

"I followed Jack McGovern. He's in the tree line a quarter mile from Director Webber's house. He's got eyes on her."

"That means he has eyes on you. If McGovern is doing deep woods reconnaissance, he's got thermal imaging, which means he can see Webber **and** he can see you, Rhys. How long has he been there?"

"Ten minutes."

"Amanda, listen carefully. If McGovern leaves right now and drives out the same way he drove in, will he pass by you?"

"No, I'm a quarter mile beyond him."

"Okay, I'm a mile from Webber's place. I'm in a black Land Rover. Give me three minutes, then put on your parking lights. When I find them, I'm gonna back in next to you. I'll park nearest to the side McGovern is on so if he sees us, he won't see your Jeep, he'll see my Land Rover. We're gonna make it look like we're necking in the woods. When I pull in, get into the back of my car, try not to make too much noise. Any way you can cover your interior lights?"

"On it." Amanda slips the straps of her bra down along her arms, wiggles free of its insidious bind, grabs a set of brass knuckles from the passenger side door pocket, puts her fingers through, takes hold of the inside cup of her bra, wraps the rest around her hand, and smacks the overhead light. "Quiet and efficient."

Jack McGovern learned about the visual into Shelby Webber's house from one of his men, but tonight is the first time he's been deep in the woods. "Fucking freezing my balls off." He stops talking when he hears his boss' voice courtesy of the bugged briefcase. "Did she just call him John? Did he just call her Shelby? A bit familiar, I'd say." McGovern sits straighter when the couple moves into view, and smiles wide when Shelby takes hold of John's hand. "There's **no way** they think they're under surveillance—" He stops cold at the sound of a car door closing, turns the viewer and scans the woods. "A Land Rover? What the ……. are they doing it out here? Get a fucking room, asshole."

As soon as Amanda's ass is inside Mike's Land Rover, he pulls her beneath him. "Stop moving," he growls.

"Get off of me." She tries to wriggle out from under him.

He wrangles, then goes all dead-weight on top of her, crushing her girly bits against his steely bits, "Amanda, stay beneath me. We can't let him see you. He knows you."

She tries to wriggle free again, "He probably knows you too."

"Yeah, but men don't look at other men, especially if there's a chance there's a naked woman nearby. So quit moving!"

She stills beneath him.

Their breathing synchs, their bodies touch in rhythm.

An image of Annie flashes through Mike, a touch memory of her beneath him pushes—he r.e.s.p.o.n.d.s. in a very unfortunate way. "I need to get off."

"Yeah, you do." She moves her hips, "Get that thing off of me."

He starts to move. He can't move. Not at **that** particular moment.

At the sound of an engine starting in the distance, Amanda pushes Mike off her chest. He pushes himself the rest of the way and starts right in. "Agent Rhys. Should you be pulled from this assignment?"

"I can't imagine I won't be," she says as she rights herself from the up close and personal security work with Specialist Monopoli.

"Agent, I asked you **if** you should be pulled from this assignment?"

"No, sir."

"You made some serious mistakes. The biggest was forgetting that you and I are partners. You **never** go anywhere without your team member knowing. You **never** follow a target into a dead end situation. Agent Rhys, we'd be here all night if I listed all the mistakes you made." Mike quiets a minute and eyes her. He's surprised to see some resolve still there. "You made some good moves, too. You parked beyond where McGovern set up, so unless he went out a different way than he came in he wasn't likely to find you. You found a weakness in Webber's security, a different one than John Maxwell found, which gives me the opportunity to tighten things up. Next time, Agent, and there better not be a next time, but if for some reason you follow a target into this type of situation, don't stop. Follow them to their location and keep going. Understood?"

"Understood."

"Another thing, Agent Rhys, don't get any ideas from whatever the hell that was. I've got a woman."

"As do I, Specialist Monopoli."

Mike smiles wide, "You're gay?"

"Lesbian, although after tonight, I may have to register as bisexual with LGBTQ headquarters."

Sex with Caligula.

John lays a fire in Shelby's bedroom while she heads to the shower. Though not invited, he joins her.

She smiles, "I was hoping you'd come."

"That's the plan, but you first." He steps toward her—she steps back until she is tight against the wall. He touches, he presses, he kisses, he whispers, "It's been too long," and he attends to all the right places.

Shelby's breaths are short and quick, her need sufficiently built, "John, please."

He sweeps back wet hair from her face, and holds her head still against the wall. He enters her bit-by-teasing-bit.

She rocks her hips forward, downward, upward, eager to take the length of him, "John, please." Shelby runs her hand down his back, across his ass as she tries to push him deep.

He only gives her what he wants to give, though he's deep enough and perfectly positioned that she begins her journey toward satisfaction. Her panting becomes broken by choppy gasps for air, her mewing is replaced by sustained moans, her eyes hood and lose focus.

He presses her tighter against the wall and buries deep, "Shelby."

She's off in her own sensations.

"Shelby, look at me. I want to watch you." John feels the beginning of her orgasm. He stops moving.

She moans in pain, "Please. I..."

He moves deeper, "Shelby, look at me."

She finds his eyes as the beginning of strong waves pulse and she tightens around him.

He stares deeply, then tilts his head back as he gives her all he's got to give.

The satisfied lovers sit by the fire sharing a glass of wine. John feels a shift, a distance from the woman in his embrace. "What's on your mind?" The question is met with silence. He kisses her cheek and whispers, "Shelby, if you have something to say, just say it."

"I have something to say and something to ask. Your preference?"

"Say, then ask."

"I thought you'd be more self-motivated in the sexual arena."

"I believe the word is selfish, and I usually am."

"Explain." Shelby laughs when she slips into Director Webber mode.

"I cannot explain my sexual habits without mentioning my sexual partners, Shelby."

"Proceed."

John smirks and proceeds. "Kitt and I were high school sweethearts. We conceived Annie in the back of my father's Bronco, then conceived Callie next to an empty Tequila bottle when I was pissed at Joy. My actions toward Kitt, sexual and otherwise, were fueled by an immature selfishness. There is absolutely no reason why the wonderful Kitt Mahoney should have considered a long-term relationship with me, nor is there any reason for her to have forgiven my many transgressions. It's because of who she is that we found a path to a very strong, non-sexual, loving partnership." He buzzes a few kisses along Shelby's ear, then breathes in the freshness of her showered hair. "You smell great."

"I smell like rain."

"What?"

"Haven't a clue, but that's the fragrance of my shampoo."

He breathes again, "You do smell like rain, a spring rain." He shakes his head, "I'd appreciate your never repeating that sentence, or at the very least, that you not assign it to me."

She laughs, "No one would believe me, anyway."

He kisses and breathes in again. "As for Joy, everything about our relationship was unconventional, to say the least. For the most part, we spent nearly every day of every year away from each other, so when we reunited, every minute, hour, and day was about making up for lost time. Self-motivation was really all we had. It was a case of—you're here, I'm here, tomorrow we won't be here, so let's get on with it." He shifts a bit beneath Shelby, puts a bit of distance between them, and silences for a minute of reflection. "As for Leavy, I would rather not discuss her other than to say that my ego was satisfied by my relationship with her."

Shelby turns and touches the scar on John's cheek, the one left by his recent fisticuffs with Manuel, "Are you sure you didn't feel something deeper for Leavy?"

He places his hand over hers, "That scar is apt payment for my bruised ego, nothing more."

Shelby waits through a healthy pause, "And Roni Shields?"

John scoffs, "You've done your homework I see."

She gives a little laugh, "Before you tell me about your thing with the Halle Berry lookalike, I'll go on record saying, I get it, I totally get it. I'm quite sure I'd hit the sheets with Roni."

John cracks up laughing. "Yeup. Roni's a beautiful woman, and we might have made a go of it, but the timing was way off. We got together when she came face to face with the fact that she would never have Fred Serpico in her life or her bed again. She needed something—someone—to do while she got over him. I was a willing partner in her quest to exorcise the ghost of the man she loved."

"So you were just helping a girl out?"

"And fucking with Serpico a bit," John laughs.

Shelby shakes her head, thinks about not saying what's on her mind, ultimately decides to take John's suggestion to not hedge. "I don't understand how the men of RFI handle the interchanging sexual partners. I can sort of understand how the women do it, but the men— **you men**—are the subspecies known as The-He-Man. Don't you wonder about copulatory comparison?"

"Until this very minute, no."

She laughs.

He snuggles her close. "Shelby, I don't think about the sex part of things. I just know that Kitt and Fred are perfectly suited to one another, and I would never deny Kitt happiness, or Fred for that matter. He is the good guy in just about every story ever told, even by me. Kitt Mahoney deserves a good guy, and she found him in Fred Serpico. As for Joy and Rocco, he is the only man on the planet who could get that woman to find balance. No disrespect to Joy, but she needs someone determined enough to conquer her power base. Her quest to become the preeminent cyber huntress came at the exclusion of everything else. When Rocco Fiancetti walked into her life, he expected equal billing, and he got it. The Italian and I have had our issues over the years, mostly professional in nature, and though it took time for me to accept them as a couple, I know Fiancetti is Joy's equal in every way. As for Leavy and Manuel, they have been in love and lust with one another since he pulled her from a steel drum. They should have been together from Day One, and they need to be together now. That's why we need to reunite them."

Shelby turns her head and manages a kiss to his chin.

He returns the favor to her cheek.

"Shelby, I know you think we are all part of The Compound of Caligula, but if you remove me from the mix, you've got Kitt and Fred, Joy and Rocco, and Leavy and Manuel."

Shelby spins from the V of his legs and faces him straight on, "Oh. My. God. It's not The Compound of Caligula. It's just you. **You're Caligula**. I just had sex with Caligula."

John pulls her beneath him, "And you're about to have sex with him again."

Big-ass boulders and building blocks.

Fred makes an early call, "Hey, Penny, I've been trying Ted's phone. Is he around?"

"Haven't seen him since dawn. He's not answering my calls either. I'm about to put his picture on a milk carton."

Fred laughs, "With that mug, that carton is destined to stay on the shelf. When he shows up, tell him I'm at 275. We need to get our shit in gear and find Leavy."

"Will do. Hey, Fred, should I be worried? Ted did a disappearing act yesterday, and again today. It's not like him to put distance."

"Last time I talked to your man, he was on a thinker."

"What the hell's a thinker?"

"He's pulling a shitload of threads on a topic. Right now, he's thinking about doing some damage to the person who hurt his woman. He needs to bang some shit around in his head so that he ends up on the right side of things."

"Should I be worried?"

From over her shoulder Ted answers, "No Lucky, you shouldn't be worried."

Penny disconnects from Fred.

Shelburne

Kitt and her toddler son, Joseph, are on their daily trek through the woods surrounding the main perimeter of The Compound. They've been gone a good measure of time, which means Steve can't do his sniper work until she gets back. From over his shoulder, Maura calls out, "Steve, have you seen Kitt? She's supposed to watch the twins. I'm on shift with Manuel in a few minutes."

"She and Joseph are on a trek, but they should have been back by now. Maura, call Rocco. Have him shut the firing range for the rest of the day. I'm going to go look for them."

Kitt pulls Joey close, "Shhhh. You can't talk when you're playing Hide 'n Seek, Joseph." She presses her back tight against a big-ass rock, and strains to listen. *Footfalls. Two sets? Coming from* ……. Her heart races when she hears Steve's call coming from the opposite direction. She waits until she's sure, "Steve, over here."

He runs full-out, "Kitt! Where are you?"

She takes her orange skullcap off and waves it high. "Here. Over here."

Steve rounds the boulder.

She keeps up the charade, "Oh, Joey, Steve found us. What a fun game of Hide 'n Seek." She shakes her head toward Steve and points,

"Someone. Two, I think. They ran when they heard or saw you coming."

"Kitt stay where you are." He raises a finger to his lips, moves behind a tree, closes his eyes and listens. He shakes his head, "Nothing." Steve calls Rocco, "I found Kitt and Joseph. Do a headcount. See if any recruits are unaccounted for. Kitt said two people were in the woods and moving in her direction. She and Joey hid behind the boulder at acre 22. I'm sending them in."

Steve takes Joey and offers Kitt a hand up. "You need to carry him, okay?"

"Okay."

"Keep Joey in front of your body."

"Okay."

"Walk toward the Main Cottage. I'm hanging back here. Whenever you come to a big enough tree, use it as cover before moving on. Be as quiet as you can, Kitt."

The very unnerved mother pulls her son close to her chest and moves out. At acre 13 she meets up with Rocco and Joy. "Give Joey to me, Kitt," Joy instructs, while Rocco moves deeper into the woods.

275

Fred has barely stored his gear at 275 when he receives a call from his best friend. "Steve Phelps. How goes—"

"Don't say shit about the interruption. First off, Kitt and Joseph are fine."

"They'd better be fine—what the fuck, Steve?"

"They were late getting back from their morning trek, so I went looking for them. I found them sheltering behind the boulder at acre 22. Kitt told Joey they were playing Hide 'n Seek, but she'd actually sought a hiding place from two people moving through the woods toward her."

"What did you find?"

"Rocco and I did a trek. There are footprints in the snow cover beyond where Kitt and Joey were. It looks like the breach onto RFI property happened at the bridge that crosses Roseway River. There are tire tracks on the other side and some evidence that someone might have set a lookout across the way. Could be hunters, Fred."

"What about recruits?"

"All but five were at The Compound. Those five left for the U.K. yesterday. Rocco's working with Mick Bentley to make sure they are across the pond."

"Kitt?"

"She's mostly okay. She and your boy have been warming up in front of a fire and are building skyscrapers with blocks."

"What do you mean she's mostly okay."

"She's got the shakes, Fred. Today might have dug up the Charles Eaton Alden shit."

"Is the jet available?"

"It's on its way. ETA two hours."

"Thanks, partner." Fred grabs his jacket and leaves 275 through the back exit. He's across Merchant Street and in Hufnagle Park for a couple minutes before he sees Ted and gives a holler, "Brothers!" The early morning shoutout garners every set of eyes his way.

Penthouse
Malcolm Price leans over the back of the couch upon which his very pregnant wife, Gretchen Mitchell relaxes. "I'm heading out, Woman."

"Uh huh."

"You doing good, Gretchen?"

"Uh huh."

He follows her line of sight, "What's got your attention?"

"Fred and Ted are in the park. Something's up."

Malcolm joins the snoop fest, "Fred's a bit animated."

"Uh huh."

"Not used to your abbreviated communication, Woman."

"They're heading this way. Go downstairs and see if everything is okay."

The ping of the privacy elevator at ground-level is in sync with the closing of the garage door. Malcolm approaches, "Gretchen sent me to see what's going on. She spied you two from her perch and decided something's wrong."

"I'm heading back to The Compound to check on Kitt and Joseph."

Malcolm leans back against Ted's Land Rover, "What happened?"

"There were unwelcome visitors at The Compound. Kitt heard them when she was on her morning walk with Joey and took cover."

"There's more?"

"Steve thinks the event unearthed some shit from the Charles Eaton Alden stalking and shooting event. Ted's gonna take me to Fox Hollow. I'll be back for a team meeting tomorrow morning at 10. Any chance you could—"

"I'll be there."

Why are you here?

Fred watches Kitt loop the track at the Athletic Center for a couple minutes before entering. He takes a seat on a bleacher bench, puts his elbows onto the one behind him, and stretches his long legs out in front. He tries to make eye contact with Kitt when she rounds the far end of the quarter mile track. She averts his stare, her facial expression tightens, her body pushes its limits. She passes by without so much as a look his way. On her fourth loop, he gets off his duff and jogs diagonally across the track, arriving seconds before she rounds the far corner. She makes a move to round him. He cuts her off.

"Move," pant, pant, pant, "Fred."

She bobs.

He weaves.

"Kittridge, stop." He takes hold of her wrist. "Stop."

"Why are you," pant, pant, pant, "here?"

"Why are you punishing yourself?"

She shakes off his hand, "Steve shouldn't have called you."

"Yeah, well he did."

"He should mind his business."

"Yeah? And me?"

"You should mind your business, too." She swipes at sweat along her brow and steps around him.

He lets her. When he gets to the exit, he calls over his shoulder, "You're pregnant, Kittridge."

She stops running at the sound of the slamming door.

Candace Hayes, an FBI agent and physician's assistant assigned to Manuel's medical team finds Kitt sitting on the floor of the women's locker room. She tosses her duffle into a locker and takes some space near Kitt. "The floor's kinda cold. How long have you been here, Ms. Mahoney?"

"Kitt."

"How long?"

"Not sure. Maybe an hour."

Candace takes Kitt's wrist and checks her pulse. "Are you hurt?"

Kitt scoffs. "Just having a bad day, Agent Hayes."

"Candace."

Kitt pulls a breath. It's one of those choppy kind of breaths that linger after a good long cry.

"I overheard Maura say you're pregnant. Are you upset because…"

Kitt interrupts her, "The baby is fine. I'm fine."

"Are you sure about that?"

"No, I am not fine. I'm pissed." Kitt pushes herself from the floor and starts pacing the length of the room, slamming closed a few lockers along the way. "I'm pissed that I cowered in the bitter cold today instead of taking action. I'm pissed that I had to be rescued by Steve, and Joy, and Rocco. I'm pissed that Fred flew back to – to – to, I don't even know why he flew back. I'm pissed that I can't kill Charles Eaton Alden again!"

"You need to sit down."

Candace joins her on a bench and takes her pulse again. "Kitt, I want you to concentrate on some slow breathing. Okay. Good." After a few minutes, the nurse practitioner slides out of that role and into the role of Agent Candace Hayes. "I'm gonna take apart your rant, okay."

"Okay."

"I heard what happened today. First point: you did take action. You found a safe place for you and your toddler. Second point: you are part of a law enforcement team. When one of us is in danger, we act. Steve, Joy and Rocco did not rescue you, they assisted you out of a dangerous situation. Third point: Fred flew back because he loves you. Fourth point: you killed a man? You killed Charles Eaton Alden?"

"Yes."

"Self-defense?"

"Yes."

"You shot him?"

"Yes."

"Are you having flashbacks?"

"Yes."

"Just today?"

"No."

"When else?"

"Whenever I hear shots from the firing range."

Candace wraps her arm around Kitt, "That's a lot of flashback activity."

"Yes."

"How can I help?"

"Weapons training. I want it. I need it. And I don't want to do it with my friends or family."

"Done. We'll start tomorrow. Before you head back to the Main Cottage, I want to check you out at the medical suite. You've had a hell of a day, Kitt."

"I'm starting to feel it."

"I bet."

PA Hayes does a workup on the pregnant Kitt then leaves her in an exam room with the promise to return in a minute. Within that minute, the patient drifts off to sleep. The PA makes a phone call. "Detective Serpico, this is Agent Hayes. Kitt is with me at the lower level medical unit. She's had an emotional response to today's event and is currently resting here. I think you might…"

"Where is she?" Fred asks from the doorway.

Candace laughs, "That was fast. She's resting in there. You can go in, but do not disturb her. Got it?"

"Got it." Fred moves quietly into the exam room, leans against a wall, and takes in the beauty of Kittridge Anne Mahoney. He exhales the breath he'd been holding for hours and bangs their recent conversation through his head. He stops when he gets to the question she asked, the one he never answered. He answers it now, "I'm here because I love you."

Kitt stirs. "I know you love me, Fred, but I need you to leave. I need to work through something on my own."

He pushes off the wall and takes a seat on the edge of her bed, "Work your way through something—or away from something?"

"I don't know."

He takes her hand. She threads their fingers together. "You need to leave."

He kisses her hand. He walks away.

Tilt-a-whirls and torched wheels.

Fred is back at 275 and ready for the 10 AM meeting. Before it starts, he spends some time riding the leather couch with Gretchen who has her swollen legs on his lap and a hand on her baby ball.

"Everything okay, Gretchen?"

"The baby barely moves. I'm a bit concerned."

Fred gently pats Gretchen's legs, "DelRae is fine. She's just a bit cramped is all and she's resting up for the big event. Joseph did the same thing—it freaked Kittridge out even though she'd been through it with Annie and Callie."

"How is Kitt? Malcolm mentioned—"

"She's setting herself right."

"Good for her."

"Yeah." Fred moves to get up when he sees Malcolm approach. Gretchen squeezes his hand, "It's good for you, too, Fred."

He smiles wide at Gretchen then nods at Malcolm's spinning hand. Each man takes hold of the couch and spins it so it's facing the living room. The soon-to-be-mommy squeals with delight and is rewarded with a tumbling roll from DelRae, "That's just what she needed, Fred. A little tilt-a-whirl."

Fred kisses the cheek of the relieved momma and gets to work. "We are going to do a Round Robin. I want updates on every damn thing going on in this investigation. Before we start, there are a couple things you all should know. First, Manuel has turned the corner. He's out of bed, on his feet, and ornery as a bear."

There are hoots and hollers, and from Gretchen there are tears.

Fred winks her way and moves on, "He's filled in the missing pieces from that day, and these are the facts as he relates them. Mathis Reynolds shot Manuel in the back, and Eli Reynolds kidnapped Leavy. Those are no longer assumptions boys and girls." That news is put to rest with the clap of Fred's hands, "Okay, let's just go around the circle, cyber review is first."

Randy

"I'm working the poisonings of Dominique Brettenvue, Dan Shea, and Paul Ferraro. Let me begin with the threads that bind these poisoned prisoners. Their last suppers were without bread and wine, but each meal contained tainted taters laced with tetrodotoxin, also known as TTX. A few bites of the spiked spuds caused paralysis to the muscles of the diaphragm and chest wall which lead to respiratory failure."

Peyton raises her hand eager to get in on Randy's lecture. He laughs at her polite interruption, "What's up babe?"

"Rosa Klebb, the assassin in the James Bond movie *From Russia With Love* used TTX."

Randy nods, "But Klebb's TTX was generated from the pufferfish. In this case, TTX most likely came from ...." Randy waits until Peyton figures it out, then they say in unison, "The blue-ringed octopus."

"Hot damn," Peyton enthuses, "that menacing mollusk is all over this case."

The 275 audience gives it up for the Randy and Peyton Show with an enthusiastic round of applause which Randy silences.

"There's more, so settle down or I'll be forced to go all Fred Serpico on you." He ignores the growl coming from Fred's direction. "Now for the differences. Dominique Brettenvue was in solitary confinement in a woman's Federal penitentiary in Lewisburg, Pennsylvania. Dan Shea was in a protected area at MCI-Cedar Junction maximum security prison in Walpole, Massachusetts. And Paul Ferraro was being housed at the DC Correctional Treatment Facility, a rather cushy place to land given the plethora of charges hanging over his head." He bounces to his feet and goes to a whiteboard. He explains along the way.

"These vastly different places of incarceration have one thing in common, they receive prisoner foods from the same national food preparation service. The way this system works is the prisons decide what they want their prisoners to eat, and they make their requests either online or with a telephone customer service representative. The food service provides distribution on a national level, either directly to the prisons or to local distributors. Once the food is at the prisons, it is handled by the commissary. When Fred gave me this assignment he asked for a deep dive on the personnel who work the food handling and distribution at the prisons, particularly anyone who may have mysteriously disappeared after the inmates' deaths." He begins writing.

"Curt Sanders: Until very recently, Mr. Sanders was a commissary worker at the Federal penitentiary in Lewisburg. He retired two weeks after Dominique's death, broke his residential rental agreement, and left for places unknown.

"William Phillips: Until very recently, Mr. Philips was a commissary worker at MCI-Cedar Junction. An exemplary employee for more than a decade, he inexplicably picked a fight with a prisoner a few days after Dan Shea's poisoning and was relieved from duty pending a disciplinary hearing. Rather than go that route, Mr. Philips quit on the spot. He has subsequently left the Bay State for places unknown.

"<u>Carmella Nuñez</u>: Until very recently, Ms. Nuñez was a commissary worker at the DC Correctional Treatment Facility. She was killed in a car accident the day after Paul Ferraro died by venomous veggie." Randy ignores Fred's groan. "Detective Serpico, if you need to ponder the whereabouts of Colonel Sanders and Will-Phil, the windows are right over there."

"Don't need the window for a ponder, but might use them for a jump. In the meantime, see if there are any trails on Sanders and Philips. We don't want to make contact at this point, but we don't want them unmonitored either. And find out everything you can about the accident that resulted in the death of Carmella Nuñez." Fred turns his attention to Peyton, "Anything to report, Madam Justice?"

"Negative."

"Okay, military review is next."

Penny

"Fred put me on identifying the newest Realm sniper. I asked Randy to tweak the program Leavy used to ID Paul Ferraro to include ex-military women, aged thirty to forty-five, from all branches of service. The search isolated seventeen servicewomen with advanced sniper capabilities. We ran those seventeen names through Leavy's computer program that links ex-military members to survivalist communities and training schools. Our seventeen possibilities were whittled down to three. Using geography as the final data point, our three possibilities were then whittled to one."

Penny stops for a minute. By the time she continues, she's wearing a big-ass smile. "Boys and girls, The Kid and I believe our female assassin is Layne Osterman of Beaver Falls, Pennsylvania."

Ted

"Beaver Fucking Falls," he says as he pushes himself from the floor. "Sorry, Lucky, but I need into this conversation right now. Some of you know that I disappeared for several hours yesterday. I was in Philadelphia having a not-so-friendly conversation with my CO and Internal Affairs."

Fred is all ears.

Ted continues, "The conversation was a preliminary 'let's get this fucker on the record' about Kelly Thompson's murder—and since he's here let's squeeze him about the Mason Trellis killing. I didn't take kindly to the grilling, so I turned in my badge, quit the force, told them to arrest me or contact my attorney, Granger Mitchell, to arrange an appointment to speak with me."

Ted smiles wide, "I'm sure you already surmised this, Gretchen, but the mere mention of your father's name shut them the fuck up."

She laughs. "I suspect it did, as well it should."

Ted laughs. "Damned satisfying, I tell you. Anyway, back to matters at hand. When I was driving here, I got a call from Philly PD Officer Landry. He said he remembered a cherry red Camaro on my street recently. He didn't make much of it at first, but after Kelly Thompson's murder, he said he got a hinky feeling that the driver might have been casing my place. He did a search of boosted cars and got a hit. A cherry red Camaro was stolen from a neighborhood not too far from Granger Mitchell's place on Old Estate Road, on November 5th."

"Election day," newly seated Mayor Price offers.

"The day Celia Brettenvue was murdered," Fred adds on, then tries to continue on.

Ted stops him, "I'm not finished, Serpico."

Fred laughs, "Then finish, Brothers."

"Landry said he saw a report the other day about a torched vehicle with a body inside. He said he got another hinky feeling." Ted smiles w.i.d.e. at his partner. "Ask me where the car and bones are located, Fred."

The detective laughs big. "I'll play along, Detective Brothers. Where's the car with the bones?"

"Beaver Falls, Pennsylvania."

Fred is on his feet moving and thinking. This go around, he doesn't even need to stare and process. "Benton Brettenvue," is all he says.

Ted nods, "That's my guess."

"Okay, let's take a break. I need to—"

"Process," the crowd offers.

One step forward—

Fred has been at the windows overlooking Hufnagle for nearly an hour. It's been snowing lightly all day, but over the past hour the intensity has picked up.

Ted joins the detective. "Weather reports are calling for two plus feet."

"Of?"

"The white stuff falling and accumulating outside the window you're standing in front of."

"Yeah … Right. I'm gonna run something. I want you to jump in when you find a hole."

"You want me to interrupt?"

"Yeah."

"That's some new shit."

"Yeah. Okay, Benton Brettenvue was questioned by the FBI about his relationship with Peruvian crime lord, Antonio Alvarez. To varying degrees, both men have knowledge of and association with The Realm, an international crime organization. Brettenvue was released from FBI questioning and within hours was pulled into the Philly PD for questioning in the Abigail Forrester murder. He got out of there and went into hiding somewhere."

Granger joins the men at the window, "Sorry for the interruption, Fred, but Celia told me the Brettenvue estate has a panic room that's outfitted with a bed, recliner, refrigerator, a toilet and sink. He probably holed up there."

Fred nods then ponders a bit, "Okay, so Benton was released from FBI and PPD questioning, went home and got ready for a stay in the panic room. When he felt the heat was off, he made a run for it, but he couldn't drive his Alpina to places unknown, so he boosted a ride from a neighborhood close to where his soon-to-be murdered wife was staying."

Ted jumps in, "I'm good until Benton chooses **that** neighborhood to boost a car."

"Okay, let me start again. When Benton got out of the panic room, he decided to leave Philly, but before he hit the road, he went by Granger's place to kill Celia. He couldn't get past the security gate on Old Estate Road, so he moved through the neighborhood looking for a way in. As much as Benton wanted to choke the life out of his wife, he realized he couldn't get near the Carriage House. Next best thing was to boost a sweet ride from a neighborhood near Granger's for his drive into the sunset."

Ted nods, "Okay, I'm good on this point, although I want to know how he got from his estate to the area around Granger's estate."

Fred nods and continues. "Okay, we'll check that out, but let's push forward. Benton's got a new ride and maybe a trunk full of cash. Any chance he just ended up in a Podunk fishing hole named Beaver Falls where Layne Osterman, female sniper extraordinaire, lives?"

The mathematician laughs. "Statistically speaking, there's zero percent chance of that—and before you ask, there's a minuscule probability the body in the torched car isn't Benton Brettenvue."

"Thanks, Poindexter."

"Live to serve, partner. Not sure I mentioned this, but the car and bones are staying put until spring, I say we get in touch with the authorities in Beaver Falls. There's no chance law enforcement isn't going to know about an ex-military woman and what kind of car she drives."

Fred claps his hands. "Okay, everyone is on Layne Osterman. Work together folks, no need to duplicate effort."

…and two steps flashback.

Candace Hayes meets Kitt Mahoney at the indoor firing range just before noon. The FBI agent's request that no one else be at the facility was approved by Rocco Fiancetti. Candace notes Kitt's attentiveness and eagerness to learn about gun safety and weapons management. She notes her resistance to actually handle a weapon, too.

"Are you having second thoughts about this, Kitt? Kitt…"

"Hurry the fuck up, bitch." Charles Eaton Alden pushed Kitt into the passenger seat of a black Tacoma. "Move over," he pressed his gun against her ribs.

She yelped in pain.

"Shut up and drive."

Her hands shook uncontrollably, and her eyes blinded with tears. She moved the vehicle forward, and in doing so she hit the truck's tail against the car on her left. She started to cry.

"Stop crying, or I'll give you something to cry about!" he screamed. "Don't do anything stupid. Just drive to my bungalow, the one you named Bullet Bungalow, you fucking bitch. Well, it's time to make the vulgar name count for something. First a bullet for you, then a bullet for me. It all ends tonight!"

"Kitt." Candance gently touches Kitt's shoulder when she sees awareness returning. "How often do you flashback?"

"Not often."

"How long have you been having them?"

"Since May."

"What happened in May?"

"Fred was shot."

Can't un-ring that bell.

It's just before midnight when Fred calls John.

"Kinda late, Fred."

"Couldn't sleep."

"Kitt?"

"Yeah, but before we discuss Kittridge, there are some things—"

"I'll get Mike on speaker with me. Hold on." John makes his way to the basement athletic room where Mike's camping out. "We're on, Fred."

He takes no time with pleasantries, "Okay, the snow's falling hard and the shit's hitting fast at 275. We're pulling a thread on a former military woman assigned to a ranger unit connected to Eli Reynolds, Paul Ferraro, and Mason Trellis. We also have a burned body in a vehicle in Beaver Falls, Pennsylvania. Come spring when they analyze the remains, we think it'll show the bones belong to Benton Brettenvue. That's it on the business end of things, on the personal end of things, I think I'm spending New Year's Eve alone in Lewisburg."

"New Year's Eve – that's today?" John asks mystified.

"Apparently," Fred scoffs. "Any chance either of you have heard from Kittridge and maybe she said I can go to Shelburne for a little celebrating?"

"Heard about her," John offers.

"Care to share?"

"Joy said Kitt spent time with Agent Hayes at the firing range."

Fred slumps against a wall, grunts when he makes contact.

"What was that?"

"Me hitting a wall."

"You didn't know?"

"No. What do you know, Mike?"

"Annie said when Kitt isn't with Joseph she's at the Athletic Center. She's working herself pretty hard, Fred. According to Annie, Kitt isn't talking much, but she's clearly reacting to her time in the woods."

"Any news on that? There was a breach at the Fiancetti Compound. We need to know by whom. Even if it's only hunters, they still present a danger. Those woods need to be locked down."

"Rocco's on it, Fred. He made an offer on 75 additional acres across Roseway River."

"Good. Either of you hear anything else about Kittridge, clue me in. Okay, what's happening in the DC area?"

"Rhys went rogue," John tosses.

"Can't wait to hear about this, Mike."

"Rhys followed Jack McGovern from DC to a desolate road in Alexandria, not too far from Webber's waterfront place. Jack pulled into the woods to do some surveillance. Rhys followed, realized she made a mistake, and called me. Luckily, Jack was focused on John and Shelby and didn't find Rhys before I got to her. I came down hard on her and don't think she'll step out of line again. The upshoot from all this is that she uncovered a security vulnerability. The place McGovern set himself has a clear view into Webber's great room."

John pushes in. "Straight up bad news on that. Jack McGovern had eyes and ears on Shelby and me during a very unguarded moment. The fucker knows she's more than my boss."

Fred laughs. "Can't un-ring that bell. Speaking of bells, make sure you two ring in the New Year on a good note. Look, John, before I go, I want you to get in earshot of our snoops. Let them know RFI isn't going to look at the files and computers from Stacy's until after the New Year. Let the snoops think RFI is going home for a few days. If The Realm's surveillance team thinks we're gone, it will take the heat off Mike while he works security on your end. But that will mean Jack McGovern's surveillance team will be all over you and Shelby. Stay locked down, John. Another thing, I don't think you need to spend time with Roland Gaffney right now.

We're moving forward. If we hit a stumbling block we can reassess, okay?"

"Got it."

"John, I want you to listen. I have a nudge that there's gonna be a move on you. Stay put. I don't have the resources right now to protect you."

"We're staying put, Fred. I've got some plans for Ms. Webber now that I know it's New Year's Eve."

"Good, but we're only ten minutes into this day, and I feel something big is on the horizon. There's lots of time for action, John, and if you're not careful, none of us will be celebrating."

Many hours later, RFI Security Specialist Mike Monopoli and FBI Agent Amanda Rhys enter the lower level of Shelby Webber's house after doing a late evening perimeter check. "I hope you don't have plans for New Year's Eve, Rhys."

"I don't. Why?"

He raises his 'give me a minute' finger and makes a call, then hangs up after one ring. "John will be down in a minute."

It's more than a minute, and it's clear he was pulled from a Caligula-moment. "What's up?"

"Not you," Mike laughs.

John addresses his subordinate, "Agent, are you armed?"

"Yes, Director Maxwell."

"May I have your weapon?"

"No, sir."

"Agent, did you refuse a directive?"

"No, sir. You asked if you could have my weapon. I declined, sir."

"Very well."

Mike pushes in. "Look, John. My gut says something's in the works. I'm keeping Rhys here for the duration. Tell Director Webber that no matter what happens, she is not to leave these premises. That goes for you, too. It's unlikely this place can be breached, so we should expect their plan is to lure you two out. Happy New Year."

Snowfall Prison

For the first time since arriving at the cabin Leavy needs feminine hygiene products. Her heavy sigh of relief takes away the torturous attempts to count backwards to her last cycle. She's failed every time to arrange things in her head—the trauma of Stacy's death and funeral service, her own concussion and recovery at the townhouse, her kidnapping and imprisonment at some remote cabin. The vagueness of it all had left her with an overwhelming fear that she might be pregnant, so the red stain floods her with relief.

There is no baby, Manuel's or Eli's. Good. The amount of 'relaxants' and who knows what else he's been giving me would have hurt any child nestled in my womb. Thank God there's no baby. She scoffs and snarls a bit, God. Are you even out there? I believed in you, even after you took my mother and father on the same day. Even after you let Dan Shea kidnap me. But now? Why did you let Eli kidnap me? Why are you letting him abuse me? Why have you abandoned me? She is lost in thought at the loft window seat when Eli joins her.

"You have your period."

"Yes."

"I was beginning to wonder. Here." Eli hands her two pills and a heating pad. "Take the OTCs and use the heating pad, they will help with cramps."

As uncomfortable as this conversation is, Leavy ups the level. "Eli, I'm afraid I might get pregnant."

A flash of anger crosses his face, "Why is that, Leavy?"

"I am being drugged, which means that any child I carry will be drugged as well."

"Is that your only concern?"

"Yes," she lies.

Eli places his hand onto her knee, "I agree that the time is not right for a baby. You'll begin birth control."

Leavy's eyes fill with tears and her body floods with relief.

Out with the old.

Five days have passed since Mathis Reynolds left the home of Felicity Ferraro. On more than one occasion, she's feared her belligerence toward The Body will leave her dead like Paul, or missing-in-action like Turner. "Where are you, Turner? You can't be dead because **you** are the long game. It makes sense that you'd step back to run your campaign, but you've been off the grid far too long. I haven't seen a single news report that suggests you're on the trail." She pours herself a glass of wine and goes to the living room. "If I'm wondering where you are, then the Gang of Eight is wondering…" Felicity nearly jumps from her skin at the ring of her phone. "Hello," she blurts.

"Turner will be in touch when I ask him to be in touch."

Felicity's eyes scan her surroundings, "Listening? Watching?" Her questions go unanswered.

"Do you have anything to report?"

"John Maxwell and Shelby Webber know they are under surveillance. They were out of town for the Christmas holiday, and Jack thinks they were at the Fiancetti Compound."

"His fortress." The Body's usual controlled affect takes on an edge. "Realm associates, Bob

O'Brien and Dominique Brettenvue infiltrated Fiancetti's hideout in an attempt to get Joy Fiancetti, Annie Mahoney-Maxwell, and Hannah Leavy. They failed their coup d'état."

"Bold move, a coup attempt against Fiancetti from inside his own walls?"

"The coup attempt wasn't against Fiancetti, Felicity. It was against The Realm. The traitors banded with Antonio Alvarez to get the cyber huntresses with an ultimate goal of using them as leverage against The Body, who they assumed was Turner Rodgers. Their goal was to push The Body aside or join him at the top. Some of the traitors died at The Compound, others died in prison cells, others will soon follow. Unfortunately for The Realm, the dead took the location of The Compound to their graves. When the time comes, I will find Fiancetti's lair, and I will make my move. The time for that is not imminent. Please continue with your report."

"John Maxwell lives and works exclusively from Webber's waterfront property. Jack McGovern's surveillance revealed a personal relationship between the two. On another note, RFI will not be reviewing the files and computers from Stacy Remington's townhouse until sometime after the New Year. The most pressing matter for me is the Gang of Eight. They are demanding a meeting."

He disconnects.

A bit past 9 PM, Felicity Ferraro heads to her bedroom desperate to avoid the televised frivolity that ushers in a new year. She aimlessly roams the massive room, sits a moment on the club chair Paul favored, then abandons it quickly for another stroll. "A shower. Perhaps I could wash this wretched year from me. No. The shower is a lonely place now, a soggy chamber where memories and regret feel free to join. No! No more! Perhaps my resolution is upon me: no more showers!" She laughs, slumps to the corner of the bed when the sound echoes back. In that instant, Felicity Ferraro gets p.i.s.s.e.d. Really p.i.s.s.e.d.

The angry widow opts for something much more therapeutic than a cry beneath warm water. She storms to Paul's closet, pulls every damned thing from every damned hanger and tosses the lot onto the floor. She runs downstairs, grabs a box of garbage bags, and storms back to her room. She pulls bag after bag after bag, snaps each one open, and stuffs them full. When his closet is empty, she begins on his dresser. "Out! Out! Out!" she yells as she drags the bulging bags the length of the hallway and pushes each down the flight of stairs. Sweaty and puffing from her workout, she plops her ass down and tries to calm herself. After a struggle to keep the tears at bay, she wonders about her brood. "Are you well cared for? You must be missing me. Do you cry yourselves to sleep? Try not to, little ones. Try to face your fears." She drags herself upright and readies for one more task—one that involves facing her own fears, the only ones she has ever had.

An odd resonance accompanies her movements through empty bedrooms. It pushes against memories of her little ones' nightly calls for just another kiss. The recollections haunt and hollow her heart. The aching woman moves from room to room and back again. She runs her fingertips across tiny mementos, hugs tight to her chest favored stuffed animals, and pulls long inhales from sweatshirts that hang from doorknobs and chair arms. It's in the twins' room that the mother dives into the deep end of loneliness and begs for the blessing of slumber—or perhaps death. She startles at the touch of her cheek and opens her eyes long enough to have them fill with tears.

Mathis removes his jacket, lays it across her shoulders, and joins her on the floor. He gently lifts her head onto his lap and runs his fingers through long mahogany waves that are spread messily about her face and shoulders. He makes no other move. He says no words. He's already drawn his line. She needs to come to him when she is ready.

Apparently, she is ready.

"I'm going to take a shower. Please wait for me in my room."

He is sitting on the club chair near an open and empty closet. His feet rest on an ottoman, his hand holds a finger or two of scotch, his gaze is fixed on dancing flames behind a corner fireplace. And. Then. She. Steals. His. Gaze. He delights in her boldness, her nakedness as she enters the room. "Stay there." He takes a sip of his drink, sets the glass aside, pushes to a stand, and walks toward her.

She steps back from his approach until there is nowhere left to go. The cold of the wall at her back buds her nipples and goosebumps her flesh. She lifts her hand toward his face.

He takes hold—denying her touch. "I'll do the touching, Felicity." He peels clothes from his body, presses his nakedness full against her, reaches his hand between them, laying claim to what he craves, what he will fill. His length presses firm on her abdomen; his desire pulses with need. He gently squeezes her mound, moaning at its warmth. He moves his other hand toward her face, lifts her chin, and brands her with his kiss. Her breasts rise and fall on shallow breath. He cups one, gently molds it, rolls her nipple.

She moves her hand down his torso and tries to take hold of his erection.

He denies her, "Don't."

"I need—" she begs.

"I know what you need." Mathis moves his fingers to her entrance, teases her, separates her and lets them enter her, bit by bit. He moans at her wetness; he explores her depth. He quickly replaces his fingers with himself, all of him, all at once.

Felicity bucks against the wall with surprise.

He watches her face react to the pain of his length, the kind of pain that's wrapped in ecstasy. He buries himself deep and holds himself still, "Take what you need."

She moves her hips and presses against the full of him, finds the spot that will lead to orgasm—she moves again, and again, and again. When she starts to fall apart, Mathis pushes deeper and deeper. Each thrust is met with her pulsing release. Before he pulls from her, he whispers, "Don't ever become my enemy."

In with the new.

275 is quiet. The New Year was ushered in with friends and family and by a blanket of snow and layer of ice. The residents of the seventh and eighth floors have dispersed from the penthouse, leaving Malcolm and Gretchen alone. They are wrapped in each other's arms gazing at the sparkling beauty of the park that holds so many of their memories. Light from wrought iron lampposts lift sparkle from icy snow drifts on empty park benches, the picnic pavilion, and covered footbridge in the distance.

"It's like a fairytale. Pristine snow-covered land, sparkling ice, and no one disturbing the wonder of it all," Gretchen snuggles against her man.

Malcolm wraps his woman tight. "I love you, Gretchen."

"I'd say that is appropriate since I am with your child. Oh, Malcolm, I am so happy and so looking forward to meeting DelRae."

"I know, Woman." The Mayor groans at his vibrating cell. "Sorry." He reads a text. "Multiple car accident in vicinity of The Burg. Emergency personnel are heading in on foot to help the injured, plows and sanders are heading in that direction. Lights are out in 75% of Lewisburg."

The words no sooner left his mouth when Hufnagle is plunged into darkness.

702

Penny and Ted are wrapped in each other's arms listening to tiny ice chips hit the windowpane. A howling wind woke them from sleep and has left them hovering just this side of awareness.

"Penny."

"Mmmmm."

"Let's get married next New Year's Eve."

Penny spins in his arms, "That is perfect. Let's recreate the quiet of this moment when we marry."

"We can have lights though, right?"

"Candlelight."

A thunderous pounding in the hall frightens the happy planners from bed. They yank open their apartment door to find Fred and Granger simultaneously pulling their doors open across the hall. Malcolm is standing in front of them, blood staining his hands, "Fred, it's Gretchen."

An anxious group of people run single file down the length of the dimly lit hallway and up a flight of stairs. Randy and Peyton join the surge at the top landing. They all push into the penthouse. Fred and Malcom separate from the lot and head into the master bedroom. They find Mama Girl lending comfort to Gretchen. The upright, non-panting woman walks past, skims a gentle touch to each man's cheek on the way by.

Fred walks to the head of the bed, places his hand onto Gretchen's soaking forehead. "Hey, little momma, looks like it's time to meet DelRae." Fred lifts a flashlight from a bedside table and shines it near Gretchen. He focuses on her eyes—her very frightened eyes. He takes her hand, "Gretchen, you and I are going to work together, okay. I know you haven't had a baby before, for that matter neither have I, but I've delivered three little ones all by my lonesome and lots of others with help. It would be quite an honor to help you bring DelRae into this world. Okay?"

Gretchen nods and pants.

"Okay. I need to see where we are. Gretchen, I'll need my hand, okay?" She continues her death hold, "Malcolm, come hold your wife's hand. Gretchen, just concentrate on Malcolm."

The detective-turned-deliveryman pulls back the covers. The bed is wet with blood tinged amniotic fluid and the labor is very underway. Fred estimates she's five centimeters dilated. "Gretchen, I'm gonna go get cleaned up."

"Don't leave, Fred, please," she begins to weep.

"Two minutes. I promise. Malcolm count it out with her."

Fred bounds into the living room. Everyone is in motion. Researcher Randy is on the internet calling out a list of supplies needed to help in a home delivery. The women of the manor are rushing to and fro gathering those supplies. Ted and Penny are checking weather and driving conditions on their cell phones. They all stop what they are doing when Fred bounds in. He heads to the kitchen sink and begins scrubbing his hands and forearms.

"Listen up boys and girls. First, Granger, time me. I need to be back with Gretchen in two minutes. Second, Gretchen is at least five centimeters dilated. Has she said anything about contractions?"

"She's had pains in her back on and off all day," Peyton says.

"Okay, third, anyone here deliver a baby before?"

Penny's and Ted's hands go up. "Okay, Penny, you're on labor and delivery. Ted, you're on the phone getting an ambulance here. Don't forget the woman in that room is the Mayor's wife. Start now. Randy, I want you near the room, but out of sight researching online whatever Penny and I are saying to each other. If I need to ask you something, I will, otherwise just research. Start now with blood tinged amniotic fluid. Hey, Ted, 9-1-1 status, please."

"It will be at least a half-hour, closer to an hour."

Granger jumps in, "Thirty seconds left, Fred."

"Okay, Penny get cleaned up. Randy follow me and setup in the bathroom. Ted and Granger, go door-to-door asking for flashlights. Matrons of the manner, keep the coffee coming." Fred calls over his shoulder as he heads back to Gretchen, "Ted, 9-1-1 updates every fifteen minutes." Fred makes it back to the expectant mother with three seconds to spare.

"Hi, Gretchen. I found Penny out in the hall, and she's gonna work with us. She's delivered a couple babies, so things are looking up here. I'm gonna have Malcolm step away and start timing contractions." Fred motions for Malcolm to go to the other side of the bed. "Okay, Gretchen, Penny and I are going to put a couple towels under you, as we get you onto your left side."

They work on placing a dry barrier between Gretchen and the wet sheets, then Fred moves to the left side of the bed and encourages Gretchen to take his hands. He waits through a contraction and when it starts to ease, he gently pulls her while Penny helps her roll.

As soon as Gretchen is off her back and settles comfortably, a little color comes back to her face and her eyes seem more focused. Fred stays on her left side and engages her, "Peyton said that you've been having pains in your back for most of the day."

"On and off since this morning."

"What happened right before Malcolm came to get me?"

"I had intense pain in my abdomen and felt my water break. I told you before that DelRae has been very quiet lately, I haven't felt her move all day, not even tonight when I had some orange juice. Fred, I'm so scared."

He wipes a tear from her cheek as she pants through another contraction.

"Her contractions are four minutes apart," Malcolm says from behind.

"Malcolm, come be with your wife. Gretchen, your contractions are every four minutes. They're going to last 60-90 seconds. Breathe through them and don't push. Try to rest in between."

Fred heads to the bathroom to check with Randy, "Anything on the blood?"

"A tint of blood in the amniotic fluid is normal. Blood isn't normally part of the labor phase, it usually comes during the delivery phase. How much blood are we talking about, Fred?"

"More than normal, I guess."

Gretchen is handling her labor much better now that she is on her left side. She is still experiencing a great deal of pain in her back, but she is working through the contractions determinedly and quietly.

Fred waits for a contraction to ebb, then gets close to his patient. "Hey, Gretchen, how are you doing?"

"My back. It's nearly unbearable, Fred."

"I know sweetheart. Penny and I are going to lay you flat for a minute. I want to check a few things out."

Once Gretchen is on her back, Fred and Penny feel her belly. They are hoping to find it firm; they find it soft. He steps away from the bed and heads to the bathroom, "Randy get me information on sunny side up births."

Randy types, Randy holds the laptop so Fred can read, "Okay, got it." He heads back to the laboring woman. "Okay, Gretchen, this is the thing. DelRae is sunny side up, which means she's facing your belly and her back is pressing against your spine, that's why you're experiencing intense back pain. She'll find her way into the birth canal, but her position and the pains you're having are classic signs that you're experiencing what's called back labor. What we need to do is get you out of bed for a little walk and then into a squat position. A squat will help ease your back pain and might help DelRae make a little U-turn. We'll all work together to get you up. Malcolm can take you for a little stroll, and then we'll get you into a squat. I know it sounds impossible, but trust me, you'll feel so much better."

On the second stroll around the room Gretchen notices Randy sitting on the bathroom floor.

He waves.

She raises a brow. "Malcolm."

"Yes."

"Is Randall Joseph Parker sitting on the bathroom floor of my birthing chamber."

"Yes."

"Why is Randall Joseph Parker sitting on the bathroom floor of my birthing chamber?"

"Who the hell knows."

Gretchen never makes it to a squat. She doubles over on her way back to bed, and moans through a particularly long contraction that is followed almost immediately by another. The back to back events and continual panting leave her legs shaking and her head spinning.

Fred and Penny help her onto her back and do another exam. "Okay, Gretchen, things are moving along quickly. You're fully dilated, I can see the very top of DelRae's head, it's beautiful by the way, and your contractions are getting near the two-minute mark. That's when you'll start pushing."

Penny motions Fred. "I think DelRae rotated."

Fred feels Gretchen stomach, her firm stomach. He smiles wide, "Okay, Gretchen, we're moving into the home stretch. I want you on your left side until you start pushing. Malcolm why don't you sit on the bed and let Gretchen nestle against you."

Ted pokes his head in for the fourth time with a 9-1-1 update, "Should be here in ten minutes or so. Granger and Faye are downstairs waiting."

Gretchen becomes a little agitated by the disturbance, so Fred moves as close as he can, "What's going on sweetheart?"

"I can't do this. Fred, I just can't do this anymore."

"Do what? Gretchen, look at me. This is the birth story of DelRae Price. This is how your daughter decided to come into this world. You aren't doing this, Gretchen, she is. Just relax. Be with your man, and let Penny and me see you through, okay?"

Gretchen nods and nestles close to Malcolm. She wants to tell him about the wonder of the moment, about the love she feels for him, about the joys of bringing a life into the world. Instead she pants and says, "Malcolm, at this very moment I'm having an overwhelming desire to name our daughter Fred."

"Whatever you want, Gretchen."

Gretchen Mitchell is fully dilated; her contractions are less than two minutes apart and marked with an intense need to push. Less than thirty minutes into her delivery phase Miss DelRae Price enters the world. Her first cry is accompanied by tears from her parents and rousing applause from the living room.

Fred and Penny turn Gretchen and DelRae's care over to two EMTs who finally arrive. Exhausted and elated, the delivery team of Serpico and Meehan collapse onto the bedroom floor. There's some laughing, crying, shaking, and high-fiving between the two.

As Gretchen and her daughter are strapped onto a gurney, she summons the barely functioning Fred and Penny to her side. "Fred Serpico, Penny Meehan, the Mayor and I would like you to meet your goddaughter, DelRae Finley Price."

Penny nudges Fred, "How the hell are we supposed to top this day? We're only hours into a new year and we delivered a kid, and we're designated as godparents. I tell you, Fred, there's nothing that's gonna top this."

Fred smiles wide, "Maybe not top this, but Kittridge and I will be bringing our baby into the world later this year."

Penny nudges Fred again, "And Ted and I are getting married next New Year's Eve, so it looks like 2020 is going to be freakin awesome, after all."

No mystery here.

Shelby pulled herself from bed very early and is downstairs at the farmer's table chasing something in her head. She's been staring at her dark computer screen and a blank piece of paper for hours willing each to lead her to whatever it is that's taunting her. She leaves the spiteful things behind, goes to the counter and starts the mindless process of building a new pot of coffee. She empties the remains from the pot she already plowed through, empties the wet grounds into the trash, rinses the stainless steel pieces, fills the percolator with cold water, grabs the coffee from the freezer, measures the grounds into the strainer, reassembles and plugs in the pot. She is standing at the counter lost in mind-numbing thought when she feels a disturbance behind her.

She spins, "Mike, did I disturb you?"

"No, Director. Well, yes Director, you've been up for hours. Is there something wrong?"

Shelby shakes her head and walks to the workspace she set at the table, "I'm chasing something … or it's chasing me."

"Yes, Director." As soon as the green light appears on the finished pot, he goes for a mug. "Director?" he holds up her mug.

"Please, a splash of cream and a pinch of sugar." A dawning takes hold as she watches the security specialist pour and mix, "Mike, why are you walking around freely?"

"I changed up my strategy, Director. If McGovern's team is planning to get you and John outside, I want them to know that there will be four of us coming out. It's the only deterrent we've got."

John agrees as he enters the room, "A show of force from our end, such as it is, will buy us some time while they alter their plans. On that topic, Mike, if Shelby leaves this house, I'm going with, so plan accordingly. Non-negotiable." John leans down and kisses Shelby, "I missed you upstairs."

"I couldn't sleep," she smiles.

"Next time, wake me," he touches her hair as he moves by to take a seat next to her at the table. "What's going on?"

"There's something nagging me, but I can't even find a thread, let alone pull it."

"Start the process over. Don't bother chasing whatever it is, think about what happened before your chase began."

She scoffs. "I was sleeping before the chase began—actually, I was dreaming about Caligula."

Movement behind Shelby reminds her that Mike is still in the room, she throws him a grin and a shrug of the shoulder.

He responds in kind.

John smirks. "Okay, Caligula. Explain."

"He was at The Compound."

Mike interrupts, "The RFI Compound?"

John throws him a look and a warning, "Shut up or leave."

Mike raises his mug-filled-hand and silently laughs at the man who will one day be his father-in-law. Or, depending how this morning goes, the man who **may** be his father-in-law.

"Anyway," Shelby continues, "Joy and Caligula were being stalked through the forest. They made it to the Computer Center and were trying to find something she could use to protect Caligula. For some reason, I end up in the Center with them."

John interrupts her, "No mystery here, Shelby. 1) You referenced Caligula the other night when we were at The Compound. 2) Joy is currently on the team trying to protect me from The Realm. 3) Your mind meshed the two into a story where Joy is trying to protect me, and you decided to join in so nothing bad happens to Caligula." He starts laughing.

Mike, who just cannot stop himself, guffaws, "This is absolutely priceless. The Director of the FBI thinks John Maxwell is Caligula. Happy New Year to me."

Shelby joins Mike in a much-needed laugh, then pulls short when Agent Rhys walks into the kitchen area, "Did I just hear the three of you mention, Caligula?"

Shelby, John, and Mike lose it.

The Compound

Joy pulled herself from bed very early and is at the Computer Center chasing something in her head. She's been staring at her dark computer screen and a blank piece of paper for hours willing each to lead her to whatever it is that's taunting her. She leaves the spiteful things behind and goes to a clean whiteboard. She labels it <u>Loose Ends</u> and under the title she lists three names: Dominique Brettenvue, Dan Shea, Paul Ferraro. She stares at the names and is ready to begin a detailed list of knowns under each, then pulls her hand away from the space beneath Dominique's name. "I already know all there is to know about you, Dominique." She erases the name. Then she erases Dan Shea's name, "You aren't of any consequence to The Realm, so you are of no consequence to this investigation." Then she erases Paul Ferraro's name and rewrites it at the top of the whiteboard, "I need to find out about you, Mr. Ferraro, and everyone associated with you."

The Computer Center door opens from behind. Without looking Joy orders whomever it is, "Out!"

Rocco Fiancetti laughs at his wife's command. "She's on to something big if she is vamoosing the Fiancetti." He races back to the Main Cottage, takes the stairs two at a time and warns Annie, "Perilous entrance awaits at the Computer Center."

"Say no more. Any interest in breakfast?"

"As soon as I check on Manuel." The eager father bounds down the stairs to the medical suite. The room that's been his son's home since early December is empty. A panic begins.

Agent Candace Hayes approaches, "Manuel is in the gym with Dr. Weinstock and NP Jones. You are allowed in, Mr. Fiancetti, if you would like."

The fifty-one-year-old Italian Stallion sprints to the gym. As he enters, his mind is catapulted back to the last time he saw his son in this place. It was immediately after a fisticuffs row…

The men met at center ring. There were no boxing gloves and no protective gear, just two men eager for action. Mike was inside the ring with the adversaries, "Keep it clean," he warned, before stepping out.

Manuel snarled at John, "Take your best shot. I won't block the first punch because I deserve it, but know this, you won't land a..." Before Manuel finished his sentence, John delivered a blow to Manuel's left cheek. The taste of blood unleashed him. He took several body punches from John before letting loose a torrent of blows. They were quick. They were powerful. They busted up his opponent.

After several minutes, Mike and Steve jumped into the ring and separated the men. The physical assault was over—the verbal assault was well under way. "I should have killed you when you first showed up at my place with Leavy. I knew you wanted her then, and I've lived with your wanting her ever since."

Manuel smirked, "What man tries to keep a woman who doesn't want him?"

John lunged, "You son-of-a-bitch!" Mike and Steve wrangled him back.

Silence fell over the Athletic Center when Rocco Fiancetti spoke from the doorway, "That is enough. Choices have been made; fists have been thrown. Get medical attention and stay out of one another's way. Manuel, after your time at the Medical Center, see Leavy then go back to Pennsylvania. The jet will return you there tomorrow, so make your decisions with her tonight. John, decide what your future is and tell me in the morning. Mike and Steve, confiscate their weapons and don't let them near one another again."

Both men gave a beating, and took a beating. They learned the hard way that bruised egos are better healed when there are no accompanying bruised body parts.

Rocco assesses the man on the track, "He is not the gladiator who fought for his woman. He is a man who struggles with balance and walking." Rocco retreats from the room. "My son is between the rock of who he once was and the hard place of who he needs to be again. This is my son's struggle, a private struggle." The proud father heads to the kitchen and finds it's been abandoned by Annie who has left a note.

At the firing range. Fruit salad, yogurt, and granola in the refrigerator. See you at lunch. Piccolo

Rocco grabs an apple and heads to the couch near the fire. Recent words of Mick Bentley start a slow loop in his head, *"Rocco, I fear the beast of vengeance is with you again, and you are contemplating action. If you surrender to temptation you may not walk away as freely as you did when you avenged Eleni. Your son lives, Rocco. Let that satisfy the beast."*

"I found consolation avenging Eleni. I will find it again..."

Somewhere
Sometime

The MI6 trained man was on a mission— a personal mission. He stealthily moved through the shrouded night. The man pursuing him did the same, though from time to time he let himself be known. Mick Bentley wanted Alistair Duff, aka Rocco Fiancetti, to feel the weight of his intentions, so he shadowed him in lockstep. He hoped his pursuit would temper the man's need for revenge. In hushed tone Mick implored, "Forget Karras. Raise your son. Serve your country."

The widower of Eleni tired of the interloper's watchful eye, concerned over the consequence for his friend and mentor if he saw what was to come, "You should leave, but you won't. You know you cannot stop this. It is a fait accompli," he quietly beseeched and warned. The man who grieved the loss of his wife every second of every minute of every hour, used a passing bus and an opening barroom door to give Mick the slip. He moved quickly through and around groups of people answering last call. The operative ordered a shot, then stepped in rhythm with the leaving lot. He waited until Mick passed by before taking back to the street. "Sorry, old man. This is something I need to do. Alone. Andros Karras dies tonight."

Is this subject closed?

Ted Brothers places a call to Sheriff Dunn of Beaver Falls. No longer able to identify himself as a Philly detective, he introduces himself as a consultant with Rocco Fiancetti Incorporated to the sweet-sounding girl who answers the phone.

"Grandpa, Ted Brothers from RFI is on the line for you."

A gruff man with a seasoned mix of authority and impatience takes the call. "What can I do for you, Brothers?"

"I'm calling about the torched car and body, sir."

"Figured as much. What's your interest?"

"It might be involved in a case we're working. Do you know the make and model?"

"Yup, a 2013 Chevy Tahoe."

"Don't suppose Layne Osterman drives a 2013 Chevy Tahoe?"

"Not anymore, I'd say." Sheriff Dunn is quiet for a minute.

Ted knows the man is weighing whether he should say more or ask more. He decides to say more.

"Listen, Brothers, the Ostermans are a bad lot. Layne's probably the worst. She's all twisted since her time in the service. Anyway, since the torched vehicle is most likely Layne's and there's a dead body inside, it's a safe bet she killed the guy and had her daddy or her brothers dump the dead bastard and torch the Tahoe."

"You've known the Ostermans a while, have you?"

"Longer than I care to. Billy Osterman, Layne's daddy, owns Osterman's Outdoorsman, a store that caters to survivalists and backwoods folks. When Layne's in town, she does survivalist training out of the store. She's got a pretty good thing going on that end. Don't know what else she's got going, but it ain't good."

Ted hones on the words 'survivalist training' and pushes for a bit more information. "The man we're looking for went missing in November last year, any chance you had a transient show up around that time?"

"Yup, guy named Benny stayed at a little no-tell-motel at the river's edge. Took up with Layne not long after he arrived. He disappeared around the same time as Layne. He's gonna be the body in the Tahoe."

Ted already knows the answer to his final question, "Any chance you know what Benny was driving when he pulled into town?"

"A beautiful red Camaro. It went missing the same time as Layne. You find one, you'll find the other. Good luck, Brothers."

Fred's been listening to Ted's end of the conversation, "It sounds like the Benton Brettenvue piece of the puzzle is in place."

Ted nods and smiles, "And we've got the survivalist angle on Layne Osterman tied up. Let's fill Penny in."

The men leave 701. Penny leaves 702. The three amigos bump up in the hallway.

"Survivalist training," they unison.

"You know?" they ask.

"How?" they ask.

Fred raises his hand. "This unison crap has a goddamn life of its own." He gives his head a good shake. "Penny, explain."

"You already know The Kid and I linked Layne Osterman to the rangers and to survivalist communities and training schools, but she actually did training at several Intestinal Fortitude schools across the country. Your turn."

"I placed a call to Sheriff Dunn in Beaver Falls. He said Layne Osterman does survivalist training out of her daddy's store, Osterman's Outdoorsman, and that she took up with a transient named Benny who rolled into town in a beautiful red Camaro. Both of them disappeared shortly before a torched 2013 Chevy Tahoe was found with a body inside."

Penny jumps in, "Ted, Layne Osterman drove a 2013 Chevy Tahoe."

"Sheriff Dunn mentioned that, then he went on to say that Layne came back from her time in the service all twisted up, and that she most likely killed the guy and her daddy or her brothers torched the Tahoe for her."

Penny does a little two-step. "Okay, boys, shoo, shoo. I need to find out what Layne Osterman was doing **before** Benny showed up in Beaver Falls. Out! Get out!"

Fred laughs big, "Get out of where? We're standing in the damned hallway."

"Right!" She turns on her heels, pushes into 702, and slams the door.

"Lovin that woman," Fred laughs.

"Speaking of women. Have you heard anything from Kitt?"

"No."

"Is this subject closed?"

"Yeah."

The Compound

The blizzard that brought in 2020 pummeled the eastern seaboard, finishing it's assault at the far end of the Bay of Fundy in Nova Scotia. Kitt wakes to a brilliantly beautiful day, bundles for the coldest of cold, and battles a bit of snow-blindness as she pushes through thigh-high drifts on her way to the outdoor firing range. She expects to find her shooting instructor awaiting her arrival. She finds Steve.

"Where's Candace?"

"She slipped on some ice and twisted her ankle. I can take her training session—if you want."

Kitt walks past him, "No, thanks."

"Where are you going? ……. Kitt, where are you going?"

She pulls a huge fur-trimmed hood over her wool-capped head, tugs the drawstrings taught, and ignores the question.

Steve watches her push through shitloads of snow, thinks about giving her time and space, then thinks otherwise. He moves along the path she plowed, circles around and blocks her way. "What. Is. Going. On?"

She smirks, "I don't plan on discussing things with you, Steve."

"Because I told Fred about the scare in the woods."

Silence.

"Kitt. Fred Serpico is second-in-command at this facility. If for no other reason, he needed to know about the security breach."

"That isn't why you told him."

"No?"

"No."

"I'll bite, why did I tell him?"

"You may think you were informing the second-in-command, but what you were really doing was telling your friend that his little woman freaked out and had to be rescued."

"Kitt."

"Don't press me on this, Steve."

"On what?"

"On what I'm thinking." She tries to move around him.

He blocks her way and takes hold of her hand. "Kitt."

She angrily shakes him off. "I don't belong here. I have no purpose here. I've tried to build a life for myself around the detectives, spies, snipers, and computer geniuses, but this isn't a life. I'm a grown woman who has no say in any of this. Every minute of every day, every choice I try to make is dictated by others. Even going on a damned walk has to be perfectly timed and appropriately sanctioned. And now, I can't even do that, can't even carve out that little bit of enjoyment." She wipes an anger-tear from her cheek and lowers her head with a shake. "I shouldn't be here."

Steve reaches out to her.

She steps back, "When you report this little hissy-fit to Fred, please tell him I will **not** appreciate a fly-home show of support from the busy detective." She trudges away.

Don't fear me, Felicity.

Felicity Ferraro is in trouble—the 'hurt so good' kind of trouble that's left her desperate for his sexual attention. For days, Mathis Reynolds has commanded her and stripped bare her body, and her notions of sexual satisfaction. After their first time together, he lifted the 'no touch' rule, accepted her kisses, craved her passion, and submitted to her control. But in their sexual arena, it is The Body who dominates. **That** is why Felicity is in trouble.

"You're quiet." He waits, then pushes through her silence. "I expect honesty from you Felicity. Nothing else."

"I don't recognize myself when I'm with you. There is a desire that I have never had and promised myself I would never allow. I am in a bed, doing things, wanting things, from the most dangerous man in the world."

"Perhaps it is danger you desire, Felicity." Mathis pulls her to him. He lays her flat, then straddles her chest locking her arms beneath his knees. She tries to wriggle free and begins to struggle for breath, "Look at me, Felicity."

She continues to struggle.

He presses her down harder, "Look at me, Felicity. Look. At. Me."

She stops moving, but still struggles for air.

"Don't fear me."

She focuses on his eyes.

He lifts a bit of his weight from her chest.

She calms down.

He stretches the length of her. He enters her, "Don't fear me, Felicity. Not in our bed, certainly not when I am in you." He kisses her and releases himself in her deepest place. He stays in, finds the tiny space between them, and fingers her to orgasm with feather touches. On her last pulse, she silently concedes, *there is no separation between fear and desire with Mathis Reynolds.*

They dress and head to the kitchen for sustenance. He sits at the table and watches her step throughout the room. Her movements are economical, her culinary skills, obvious. She sets two plates of sautéed vegetables drizzled with balsamic vinegar and tossed with an array of spices and freshly grated parmesan. "I haven't shopped for anything more than veggies in weeks. This will have to do."

He eats. He enjoys. "Thank you. It is very good. Perhaps you will cook again when you have time to plan a menu." He reaches across the table and brushes back an errant strand of hair that has slipped from a band in back. "You are ravishing, Felicity, even more so than the first time I saw you."

She raises an inquisitive brow, "And when was that, Mr. Reynolds?"

"In 2014 at the Kennedy Center."

Felicity pauses to recall the event and the honorees. "Mmm, Sting."

He laughs, "Mmm, Al Green."

"And Tom Hanks," they unison.

She spends a pensive minute, "I was pregnant with my twins."

"Yes."

"I was with my husband."

"Yes."

"And you wanted me then?"

"And each day since."

"Is that why Paul is dead?"

"Paul is dead because he became a liability to The Realm. He knew too much, certainly knew that when you stopped going to see him, I had pulled his legal defense. The only way out of prison for Paul Ferraro was a pardon—one he would never get. He was going to sing."

Felicity becomes quiet.

"Where'd you go?"

"Aren't you afraid that Alvarez and the others will turn on you and sing. And Roland Gaffney? Do you fear him? Certainly, he knows the most about you and the organization."

"I fear nothing and no one. The Tango leaders face legal challenges, but most will see the light of day outside prison walls."

Felicity nods. "Because Dominique is no longer alive and can't testify against them, but that still leaves Antonio Alvarez and Roland Gaffney, and perhaps even Benton Brettenvue."

"Benton met his fate at a Realm safe location," he laughs, "at the hands of a woman," he laughs harder. "A fitting end to a man who abused every woman who crossed his path. Alvarez will be meeting the same fate as Dominique. Gaffney gets a presidential pardon from Turner Rodgers. I won't have a problem with Roland, unless and until Rodgers loses the race. He won't lose the race provided he doesn't have an opponent."

"Curtis Morgan." She moves her food around the plate while she ponders. "I see organizational issues and personal vulnerabilities. May I offer them to you?"

He nods.

"The structure of The Realm is transitioning. At its inception, it had the structure of an octopus: a body and eight appendages. The Gang of Eight was told then, and still thinks now, that Turner Rodgers was The Body, and they assumed ancillary positions. Due to recent events, there are two original members missing: Roland Gaffney and Eli Reynolds. One is in prison; the other is MIA. After a bit of jockeying, Jack McGovern filled Gaffney's seat, but there has been an empty seat during the past few Gang meetings."

"Eli."

"Yes. I suspect the others think his absence is related to the assassination of Stacy Remington. After all, what man wouldn't support his brother in a time of such personal loss and anguish?"

The widower smiles. "Continue."

"Having been in the same room as the Gang, I don't think they've given Eli much thought, especially since there's been a lot of other happenings: Paul Ferraro's imprisonment, Mason Trellis' killing, Turner Rodgers' pull back, and my promotion."

Mathis remains silent as she moves her food about.

After a bit of contemplation she continues, "Do you trust Turner Rodgers?"

"I trust no one."

"I suspect not. Let me rephrase. Do you trust Turner to keep to the plan? That he will keep his mouth shut about your identity, so long as it gets him into the White House?"

"Yes."

"So your vulnerabilities come from the Gang of Eight?"

"Yes."

"Particularly, Jack McGovern."

"Most notably, but there are others."

"Thorndyke and Haley."

"Yes." He smiles wide. "I've chosen well Felicity."

"Yes." She smiles wide. "You have. May I continue?"

"Please."

"It's only a matter of time before the Gang questions Eli's prolonged absence, and they start demanding answers about the organizational structure."

"Yes."

"They will demand to meet with Turner, the man to whom they think they have pledged their allegiance."

"Yes."

She tilts her head and raises a brow, "That's where I come in?"

"Yes. You will inform the Gang that Turner Rodgers is not and has never been The Body. He will be alongside to confirm it. When there is dissention and baseless threats are hurled, you will raise the sword of Damocles over each of those degenerates. I trust as their fixer you've kept proof of the murders, rapes, pillages, infidelities, forced abortions, incestuous acts, and financial misdeeds."

She nods. "Two sets."

"Here?"

"One."

"Good. Each of the leaders knows what you have on them, and unless they have willingly shared their misdeeds with other members of the Gang, which is unlikely, then you are in the position of power. Threaten to share what you have with the Gang of Eight, and then with the public-at-large. That will settle them for the short term."

"And the long term?"

"You'll tell them who the leader is."

She pulls a breath of shock. "If I tell them you are The Body, you will never be able to walk away from this, which I assume is the plan should the shit get too close to the fan."

Mathis gets up from the table and takes hold of Felicity's hand. He pulls her near, his excitement and desire hard against her. He whispers into her hair, "You won't tell them Mathis Reynolds is The Body. You will tell them Eli Reynolds is The Body."

Felicity leans back a bit and finds his eyes, "You'll sacrifice your brother?"

"Yes."

Mathis feels the increased heartbeat of the woman pressed tight to his chest. "Is that fear I feel in your beating heart, Mrs. Ferraro?"

She throws her head back in laughter, "Fear? Hardly. You should pay less attention to what's beating in my chest and more attention to what's pulsing between my legs, Mr. Reynolds."

"I've chosen very well."

Kavanagh, Monaghan, Dublin.

Joy Fiancetti has been behind closed doors for nearly a day. She needs to talk with someone, but not someone from RFI, someone from the FBI. She places an early call.

"Webber."

"Shelby, it's Joy, are you secure?"

"Yes."

"Good. I've been working something, and I could use a sounding board."

"Very well, but when we're done, I need your help with something."

The cyber huntress takes a guess. "Director Webber is there any chance you're looking at Felicity Ferraro as Turner Rodgers' replacement?"

"Yeup."

Joy laughs big, "You sound like John Maxwell."

"Oh, for fuck's sake."

"You're a goner," Joy pronounces. "Shelby, are you diving for information on Mrs. Ferraro?"

"No, I'm kicking my research old-school, why?"

"I want exclusive diving rights. If too many people start going deep on Felicity, there might be a slip up. I don't want her or anyone else alerted to our looking at her."

Shelby exhales a sigh, "Damn, I soooo wanted to compete with the preeminent huntress of cyberland—in cyberland. Look, Joy, why don't we just keep this little research project between the two of us until we get the goods on The Widow. That way no one will tip our hand."

"Deal. Since you're doing mainstream research, why don't you start. It may help me make sense of the stuff I've got."

Shelby gathers her notes and begins, "Felicity Ferraro comes from a long line of Irish activists, insurrectionists, and terrorists. Members on both sides of her family fought during the 1916 Easter Rising and throughout the thirty-year span of the Troubles. I'm sure young Felicity and her siblings were spoon-fed a hearty helping of Irish nationalist rhetoric and paramilitary stories. Her great-great-grandfather, Conan O'Brennan, was the Sinn Fein leader of the Dublin Central Branch in the early 1900s. He and his wife, Enya, died during the 1916 Easter Rising leaving behind a one-year-old son. On Felicity's maternal side, there was Fiona Flannagan, a member of the women's nationalist group, Cumann na mBen. This ballsy woman had her feet firmly planted on the front lines of the 1916 insurrection, working as a courier and intelligence gatherer and fighting alongside the Brotherhood until the bitter end. She was arrested and imprisoned in Kilmainham for nearly a year, and on her way to freedom she purportedly told the warden she'd be back. Generations later, there came Fagan O'Brennan, Felicity's twenty-seven-year-old brother. He was one of the Disappeared. It was more than a decade before Felicity's family learned he'd been abducted, tortured, killed, and secretly buried in County Monaghan."

A shiver runs Joy's spine, seconds before the shakes take hold. She drops her marker, and slumps hard against a table, "Kavanagh, Monaghan, Dublin."

"What? Joy. Is something wrong?"

She doesn't hear Shelby; she's already thinking back to one of her reunion trips with John…

D is for Dublin

He was waiting for her at the bus terminal when she arrived back in Dublin, actually, he'd been waiting for hours. "What's in County Monaghan?"

"Spying on me, John?"

"Didn't need to spy Joy, you're on public transportation."

"What I do with my time isn't for public consumption."

He took hold of her hand to stop her, "Joy, what's in County Monaghan?"

"John, I'm trying to row my boat, please don't rock it."

"What the fuck, Joy?"

She pulled her hand away. She started to say something, chose something else to say, "O, stony grey soil is in County Monaghan."

"What's the poet Patrick Kavanaugh got to do with this?"

She walked away.

"Joy!"

~

"What do we do with her?"

"We raise her."

"We've got our own to bring up, Liam. There's barely enough for our lot."

"Siobhan, she is one of our lot."

"Your brother's lot, and his wife's lot. There's family on the wife's side in the States. You could send her there. You should send her there."

"My brother is dead—his wife is dead—two uncounted casualties of the Droppin Well bombing, if ever there was. Their girl's had a tough go of it, Siobhan. Orphaned at two, and now left again by Ma's death. You'll welcome her and treat her right."

Seven-year-old, Joy Ann Watts, cried herself to sleep that night, and most others, especially the nights when Liam Watts was away from his home in County Monaghan and off in Dublin on business. That's when Siobhan Watts set things her way in her home.

"You'll be getting what I think is right, and you'll be saying nothing to your uncle. Now down you go, and no sniveling, or else I'll be takin your doll."

Joy whispered into the ragdoll her nana made her for her first Christmas in Ireland. "It's not a dungeon, Maeve. It's not a dungeon, Maeve. It's not…" She kept her tears quiet so Siobhan wouldn't take Maeve McGinty away.

The director repeats her question for the third time. "Joy. Are you still there, Joy?"

She shakes free of the memories that are trying to take hold, "I'm here. Please keep going, Shelby."

There's a pause and a resumption. "Attorney Ferraro worked for the law firm of Preston and Porter. I heard she was let go, but no official statement has been issued on the matter. Felicity is a legal phenom who fixes things for some of the most powerful men and women in the country. Her client list is shrouded in secrecy, although there's been speculation for years about who's on it. Finding out the who's who of that list has become a parlor game amongst the movers and shakers in Washington. Rumor and inuendo suggest her clients have been involved in ruinous legal, moral, and ethical acts that she's fixed. No one knows for certain how she handles her clients' problems because no one knows who her clients are and what transgressions they've committed. I've heard that to ensure absolute secrecy about their wrongdoings, these DC movers and shakers pay their legal fees to Preston and Porter with a sizeable amount going to the fixer."

"How about Senator Rodgers? Is he rumored to be one of Mrs. Ferraro's clients?"

"Given his penchant for extramarital affairs and elbow-rubbing with questionable factions, it's been assumed he was a client of hers. It sure would be helpful knowing what the fixer did on his behalf. I personally sit at the head of the FBI and have at my fingertips every imaginable resource, and there has never been a single thread to pull on Felicity Ferraro's list."

"Maybe if we pool our resources we'll find out who's on the list, and if Turner Rodgers' name is there, we'll start pulling and won't stop until we uncover his secret. Is there more on your end?"

"No, but before you get to your diving fill me in on RFI's work, post Paul Ferraro's arrest. Any news on the search warrants for his twelve franchise locations?"

"Access to his Pennsylvania and Maryland locations was approved."

Shelby interrupts, "When?"

"Yesterday. Your Agents are going in on January 6th."

Shelby pushes from her desk, "On whose orders?"

"I'm guessing, Jack McGovern's."

"Joy, I have to go. I need to find him, fire him, or kill him! As a matter of fact, I'm getting rid of every damn man who's distracting or deceiving me."

Blowups and what the fucks.

Hours later, Shelby ignores a knock on her locked office door.

"Let me in, Shelby," John says calmly, but authoritatively.

She ignores him.

"Open the damned door, Shelby."

She ignores him.

"I'll kick this fucking door down, Shelby."

She flicks the lock.

She is nearly at her desk when he storms in.

He is fuming, "Shelby…"

"Director Webber," she snaps.

"Fucking great. We're back to this?" John crosses the room and stares down at her.

She stares back, "You are a distraction. You are to vacate my bedroom. If I could evict you from my premises, your departure would be imminent."

"Shelby."

"Address me by my title, I've earned it."

"Director," John sneers, "I think you're overacting."

She barely stays in control of her emotions, "Director Maxwell, I just learned that my direct subordinate, a man who works for the Federal Bureau of Investigations and also for a criminal organization, a man who has been surveilling me for God knows how long, and most likely knows you and I are banging boots, has taken complete control of my Bureau. I intend on taking back my power and that begins with my getting back to the office, and getting you out of my bed and my life."

John's seething kicks up a notch. "You've known about Jack McGovern's duplicity for months. Learning he usurped your authority about the search of Intestinal Fortitude is bad, but manageable."

"You talked with Joy?"

"She called after you ended your conversation. She said to stress that she only revealed to me the matter than set you off and nothing else you two discussed. She suggested you might need some talking down."

Shelby crosses her arms and leans against her desk, "Joy Fiancetti may know **you,** John, all of you, but she does not know me. Once I make up my mind about something, there is no talking me down."

The. Penny. Drops. "Damn it, Shelby! You're ending us because it was Joy who told you about being bested by Jack."

Mike bolts into the office, "What the hell is going on? You two need to calm down and quiet down. Your voices are bouncing off the walls downstairs. If I can hear every damn word, so can your listeners."

John pulls a few angry breaths then addresses Mike, "Figure out a security plan for the director, I will handle my own. I'm leaving."

Shelby calls out to him as he storms through the door, "Director Maxwell you have not been dismissed."

He turns slowly and sneers, "If I still worked for you, Director Webber, I would wait for your dismissal. Goodbye, Shelby."

She remains silent.

Mike does not, "What the holy fuck. Excuse me, Director, but I need to talk him down."

There is no talking John Maxwell down. He grabs a few of his things, throws on his pea coat, wool watchman's cap, and gloves and storms out.

Fred is already on the phone when he gets a call, "Mike, I'm on with Steve—"

"Get off," Mike demands.

Fred ends his call and returns, "What the fuck?"

"John and Shelby had a huge fight. It started out as a professional issue and turned into a personal showdown. John quit the FBI and stormed out of here. There is **no** doubt the listeners got near every bit of what was said and know that he is out on his own. I can't leave the director alone. Before you jump in Fred, the professional thing that caused this blowup has something to do with Shelby and Joy. I guess RFI found out that the FBI has the go ahead to search the Pennsylvania and Maryland branches of Intestinal Fortitude, and Jack McGovern kept the information from Shelby. She freaked that her subordinate made a power play on her Bureau because she was playing footsie with John."

"Fuck. Fuck. Fuck. Okay, Mike, ask Director Webber to give RFI one hour to deal with a few things. If she refuses and makes a move to end our working relationship, tell her she needs to personally break her contract with Rocco Fiancetti before you can vacate her premises. That gives me an hour to try to pull this fuckin train back onto the tracks."

Penny and Ted walk into Fred's apartment without knocking. The look on their faces demands immediate attention, "Mike, I need to deal with something. Give me five minutes, then go talk to Webber. Call me back after that."

Fred raises his hand to Penny and Ted, disconnects from Mike, and presses a single digit. "Rocco, the fucking shit is hitting the fan from all directions. I don't have time to explain everything, but John quit the FBI and is out on his own. If Webber calls you, do not take the call until I've had time to work some shit out. On the other matter you and I discussed, I've got Ted Brothers with me, I'll put him on with you. Hold on."

Fred hands his phone to Ted, "Rocco wants you at RFI. There's no time to talk about it, just say yes and give back my phone."

Ted takes the phone, "Rocco, my answer is yes."

Fred finishes his call with Rocco, "Talk to Joy. Find out what the fuck happened between RFI's cyber huntress and the FBI's director. Sorry for any disrespect, sir." Fred hangs up.

Penny jumps right in, "Don't interrupt me Fred."

Fred tosses a 'what the fuck' look at Ted who tosses a 'don't interrupt her' look right back.

"I was sitting and stewing about Osterman being a sniper. I figured her involvement with The Realm began with her association with Paul Ferraro and Intestinal Fortitude. Then I start wondering how Paul Ferraro became involved with The Realm. I figure it's through the rangers and Eli Reynolds, so I start wondering if Osterman's association isn't through Paul, but through Eli. As it turns out, Osterman and Reynolds both had ranger-adjacent roles in the Army; she was a sniper trainer, he was a medic. I figure that's probably why they became tight with one another. Don't know why, but something connected in my head. A memory. A thought. I don't know what, but something from my trip to Washington hit. When I was digging around in Abigail Forrester's and Turner Rodgers' business, I went to the Congressional Library and looked at the 1999 roster of interns. There were several pictures of young ladies and men rubbing elbows with the Congressional leaders of our great Republic. There was one Black intern in the mix. He was standing next to Turner Rodgers in several of the candid photos at luncheons and things. I called Katie O'Brien a few minutes ago and asked her if she remembered the Black kid's name. She identified him as Eli Reynolds. Turner Rodgers and Eli Reynolds want to keep me from putting them together in 1999."

Fred claps his hands. "Penny, I'd kiss you, but your man is standing here," he winks. "Go to the Diving Center and tell Randy. The only thing I want the two of you working on is Layne Osterman. I want to know where she took her last piss and every other piss for the past year. And since you'll be knee deep in her piss, find out if there's someone else from Eli and Layne's ranger days that might be part of this. Before you do any of that, give your man a kiss. He and I are going on the road for a few days, so say your goodbyes."

Penny leans up to her man, places a quick buzz on his cheek and says, "Be safe, love you," and leaves to do her own thing.

Fred laughs, "Gotta love that girl."

"That's a done deal, friend."

Total deniability.

Shelby didn't call Rocco to remove RFI from the investigation, and she didn't reach out to John to discuss their blowup-breakup, she slept on her anger overnight, or more to the point, she tried to sleep on it. The exhausted woman drags her ass from bed before the first ray of sun, shuffles the hallway, manages the set of stairs, and makes her way to the kitchen, where she finds the lone RFI team member setting a pot of coffee. "Morning."

"Yes, ma'am, it is."

She laughs. "Not sure why I find that funny, but I do."

"Lack of sleep might explain it, ma'am."

She nods, then sips her brew. "Any chance you can administer this intravenously?"

"Sorry, ma'am."

"Alright then." She takes several more sips before speaking again. "Mike, you need to take me to J. Edgar. I scheduled a meeting with Jack McGovern."

"It's Sunday, ma'am."

"I'm aware." She takes another sip or two before finishing their conversation. "Seems like the perfect day for firing his ass."

"Yes, ma'am."

Upon the director's arrival at the Bureau, Shelby walks directly to Jack McGovern's office, accompanied by Agent Amanda Rhys and five buzz cut agents. The office door is opened without the courtesy of a knock.

Jack is on his feet before the agents step foot inside, "What the—" No other words leave Jack's mouth because Shelby Webber walks through the flank.

"Agents, confiscate former Deputy Director Jack McGovern's service revolver and shield, then escort him out of the building. If he resists in any way, place him under arrest per order of the director of the Federal Bureau of Investigation." Shelby stops Jack on his way past, "Don't leave the District of Columbia, Jack. And good luck with your other employer, I'm sure their termination of service will be markedly more painful." She turns to Amanda Rhys, "Agent, seal this office."

McGovern calls his Realm team, "Find John Fucking Maxwell! He and Webber had a falling out, he quit the Bureau, and he's out of the waterfront property. Find him, and make sure he stays the fuck away from Webber's place. If you get a chance to take the mother fucker, do it. Now, get someone to J. Edgar to pick me up." McGovern quietly rants while he paces the sidewalk, "Too bad you had a falling out with your lover, Director Webber. If John Maxwell isn't around to protect you, I'll have a much better chance at making you pay. Agent Rhys and the RFI guy will be collateral damage on this assault, but who the fuck cares. I need to get you out of the way. Your demise won't put me back at the Bureau, but it will stall the investigation into The Realm." He calms a modicum and starts the framework for his attack. "I'll need to strike before The Realm learns I've been fired. Once the bitch is neutralized, The Realm will see my value and keep me on board. If I miss the mark, I'll go off the grid—permanently."

John Maxwell watches McGovern pace the sidewalk. "Shit. Shelby fired Jack. You just forced his hand, Shelby. He's going to take you out. If he succeeds, The Realm will keep him on. If not, he's a dead man." John calculates, "McGovern can keep his firing secret for two days, tops." He answers the fifth call that vibrates in, "Stop calling me, and stop following me, Fred. Jack McGovern has every fucking tail on The Realm's payroll out looking for me and none of them have come close. If you don't stop following me, you'll lead them right to me. Back the fuck off."

"A bit testy, John. Is it woman trouble?" Fred laughs.

"Let's do this shit later. Right now, we have a problem, and I need Mike on it. I'll be back in touch."

John calls Mike just after dark. "Don't talk. Get away from Shelby and listen."

Mike steps to Agent Rhys' desk, "I need to take this call, please stand outside Webber's door." He steps into the hall, keeping sight of the inner office. "Talk."

"I've been tailing Jack McGovern since Shelby fired him. It looks like he's making a move on her tonight. He's using the same breach I've used, and he's already been on her property scoping for a shot. Looks like he's going to try to get her when she's outside, most likely when she arrives home. I'll come back to that. McGovern spent the last hour visiting three different banks, probably draining his accounts. He's at his place boxing up some stuff. He's going off the grid after the hit. If he misses his mark completely, he's probably going to be gone for good. This is our plan. I gave Fred keys to Shelby's place, he and Ted are already inside. I called Rocco this morning, and he dispatched Steve for a little sniper-shooting. I got him to the visual clearance in the woods an hour ago." John pauses before wading into the swampy end of things. "Listen, Mike. Rocco gave Steve the order to take McGovern out as soon as he steps foot onto Shelby's property. That part of this conversation should not be disclosed to the director. She will not be allowed to proceed with this plan. Is that clear, Mike?"

"Yes."

"Good. The rest of our plan depends on you getting Webber and Rhys to the waterfront property without you being seen or them being heard. I want the three of you in Kevlar, and when you get onto the driveway, you need to move the director quickly into the house. Gotta go. McGovern is on the move."

Mike ends the call, writes a note, and hands it to Agent Rhys. She follows his instructions and knocks on Webber's door, "Excuse me, Director, the package you were expecting has arrived. The courier won't accept anyone's signature but yours." After she delivers her lines, she does the universal finger to the lip and motions her to come. The two of them head to a conference room where Mike is waiting.

"Director, John Maxwell has been tailing Jack McGovern since this morning. All indications point to an attempt being made on your life when you get home this evening."

"Who will be the shooter, Jack or John?" Webber couldn't resist the question.

Mike smiles and gives her a dip of his head for her cleverness. "Jack, ma'am. This is the RFI plan. Fred Serpico and Ted Brothers are already in your home. John Maxwell will be doing circumference work. Agent Rhys and I will be providing 'close and personal' protection. Do you have comment on what I have told you, Director?"

"Proceed."

"This is our plan. Rhys will drive the three of us to your home. I will be out of sight on the floor in back. You will do nothing but small talk, remember the bugged briefcases will be with us.

When we arrive, you will wait until I get out of the car then you will stay behind me until I get you inside your home. We leave in fifteen minutes. Rhys, we all need Kevlar."

McGovern is amped. He watches the GPS as it tracks Webber to her place on the Potomac. When she's five minutes out, he gets out of his car, moves along the property line, and waits at the tree. He talks himself through his plan, "When headlights approach, I go over the wall. As soon as she rounds the corner at the back door, I take her down and whoever else is with her. Then I get the fuck out of DC."

Steve Phelps is set for the shot. His concentration is full-on. Movement at the breach point pulls his focus. He watches every placement of every hand and foot as McGovern climbs the knotted tree and moves across the limb to the wall, then as he dangles and drops inside the estate walls. McGovern immediately moves behind a tree that obscures Steve's view.

John is crouched inside the back door, the one Shelby will enter. He assesses her likely movements as he plans his own. "I'll watch through the side widow for her approach, then wait until she opens the door. Shit. Shit. Shit. There are two doors. The screen door swings outward toward the driveway. She's going to have to walk around that door before she can open the inside door. That's when she loses cover—

that's when she'll be exposed. That's when Jack will take his shot." He texts Fred and Ted. One of them is watching the entry point at the wall, and the other is watching the street.

John:	**McGovern on the property?**
Fred:	**Yes. Behind tree. No shot for Steve.**
Ted:	**Vehicle just passed house. Arriving at security gate.**
John:	**Fred, does Steve have shot?**
Fred:	**No.**

John hears the closing of two car doors, "Should be three doors." He moves to the back door, puts his hand onto the knob and eases it open. He sees Shelby round the corner of the house, followed quickly by Amanda, but no Mike. John waits, then pushes the screen door hard. The door opens wide and knocks Shelby and Rhys to the ground just as the sound of two rapid shots ring out.

Fred calls from his vantage point, "Down, shooter down!"

John bursts through the opening and drops next to Shelby. She's out cold. Mike rounds the corner and aids Agent Rhys who is conscious, but has injured her wrist. John glares at Mike, "What the fuck?"

"I told her to wait until I was out of the vehicle. She bolted the second Rhys stopped the car. I was still getting off the fucking floor in the back seat." The men seethe while waiting for the all-clear.

Fred and Ted make it across the property and surround the unmoving man on the ground. When they give the all-clear, John lifts Shelby, and Mike helps Rhys inside. As the door shuts behind them, Mike points to the assassin's bullet wedged in the screen door. "It would have been a perfect head shot, if you hadn't pushed it open."

Fred, Ted, and Steve dispose of McGovern's body in a rather unusual way, then Fred sets the rules for his partners, "Complete deniability for the FBI director and agent."

"Sure helps that one of them is unconscious," Steve jokes.

Is in the house!
Is in the race?

Senior Senator Curtis Morgan of the great state of Georgia and his wife Madison are at 275 awaiting the arrival home of the mayoral family. With them are Granger and Faye Mitchell and Bertha King Price. The eager grandparents are standing at corner to corner windows overlooking Hufnagle Park. Each has remarked on the shoulder to shoulder group of spectators and reporters braving the bitter cold to welcome home DelRae Finley Price. Many minutes pass before a lifting sound comes from the street below. As Malcolm's Land Rover inches past the celebrants, hoots and hollers raise, several balloon bouquets lift, and chants of "78, 78, 78" call out. Malcolm stops his vehicle, and at the tail end of another round of "78, 78, 78" shouts, the former Spurs player answers back, **"Baby Price in the house!"** The crowd goes wild; 78 sleeps through it all.

The ping of the privacy elevator on its descent, and the sound of its ascent beckons near the very eager grandparents. Wide smiles and beating hearts mark the auspicious occasion.

Malcolm and Gretchen enter their family home. The MAN's protective arm is wrapped around his wife and hers cradle their child. There is utter silence welcoming them.

Gretchen smiles at the mute-brigade and whispers, "She's awake."

Oohs and aahs ensue. There is hand-shaking and shoulder-slapping amongst the men and soft touches and hushed coos from the women. The new mother smiles warmly and patiently waits through three rounds of "isn't she beautiful," then excuses herself. Gretchen Rae Mitchell walks to the group of men, locks eyes with the man who raised and guided her—who loved her above all else, "Daddy, would you like to hold your granddaughter?"

"I can't think of anything in this world I would like more," he beams.

Grandfather takes granddaughter for a stroll the length of the room, eventually ending their little trip at the wall of windows. He stands for several minutes staring into the eyes of the little girl who already owns his whole heart. "One day, my little one, I will tell you of your namesake, Miss Delaney Rae Hamilton Mitchell. A spirited young woman who brought to this world a most spirited child. That child's name is, Gretchen Rae Mitchell, and she is your mother." He leans low, "I say your mother was a spirited child, but the truth is she was quite the pisser, as is often remarked upon by a man named Fred Serpico. Oh, Miss DelRae Price, have I stories to tell you." He places a tender kiss upon the baby's forehead, then raises her until they are cheek to cheek, "I love you completely."

Gretchen joins her daddy and baby for a private moment. Words are shared and tears are shed. The new mother takes her baby and whispers, "Tell Grampa there's someone very special waiting to meet you." The two stroll slowly back to the welcoming committee. "Baby Girl, this is Mama Girl, the most wonderful mother of your daddy. If I do half as good raising you, Baby Girl, then you will grow up right fine." Gretchen places the beautiful black haired, blue eyed wonder into Mama Girl's arms.

The woman known for keeping tears to herself, moves a few away from her cheeks and a few from the new mother's. "Now you go set yourself on that deep couch over there, Gretchen. I stood in this room and heard the birthing of this baby. You need to be off your feet. Malcolm escort your wife while the grandparents of Baby Girl get their fill."

Daddy and Mommy do as they are told.

After a light lunch, Gretchen and DelRae head for a nap. Faye Mitchell, Madison Morgan, and Bertha King Price set themselves in DelRae's playroom reading greeting cards and notes sent from around the world. Poetic pieces, words of wisdom, and adages of days gone by fill the pages. True to form, it's Mama Girl's words that bring meaning, "The growing of a family is a wonderous thing. The blending of this family is a right fine miracle."

Malcolm Price, Granger Mitchell, and Curtis Morgan hole up in the mayor's home office where talk turns from babies, bottles, and burping diapers, to politics, polls, and pundit predictions.

"Ten months until the election," Malcolm addresses his father. "Your polls look strong. Any movement on the other Democratic candidates?"

"Jim Morrisey will hold on the longest. He's got the money, and he wants to sully me up a bit. He's really interested in 2024, so he's mostly setting the stage for his future run. The others are having trouble raising money, but I suspect most will all make it to the next debate."

"Any thoughts on a running mate?" Granger tees the ball.

"Too soon for me to choose, but the Democratic National Committee has their guy." Curtis drives the ball.

"Who?" Malcolm asks.

"You," they unison. They're on the green.

Malcolm laughs. He's the only one who does. "You can't be serious?"

Curtis leans back in his chair and steeples his fingers. His stare is serious, contemplative, "They think you and I are unbeatable."

Granger gets up and heads to Malcolm's wet bar where he pours a splash of single malt whiskey into each of three glasses. He hands one to his son-in-law, the other to the senator, raises his glass, and drains it, "You're mayor, you want to be governor, then what? Is that as far as your mind has taken you?" The senior men recognize the flash in Malcolm's eyes, the almost indiscernible shake of his head. Granger smiles a knowing smile, "Your reaction proves your mind has taken you all the way. This is a pathway, Malcolm. If you choose not to follow it now, you may find roadblocks later. Think about it, son." Granger puts his glass back onto the bar and readies to leave, "I think the two of you have things to discuss."

Close and yet so far.

Fred and Ted drag their exhausted asses to Shelby's house late the next day. They've been with the recently departed, Jack McGovern, since the time he departed. John Maxwell's been walking the floors that whole time. The usually calm, cool, and collected man snaps when the men return. "What the fuck took so long?"

Fred laughs, "Good afternoon to you, too, Jackass. We had some packing and shipping issues, then we spent time in Jack McGovern's place. We left the impression that the former deputy director is on the run. While we were there, we did a thorough examination of his files, took what we wanted, and borrowed a few computers he had in the trunk of his car."

"They can't come in here," John stresses.

"They're already en route to their new home in Canada. Steve will have a lot less trouble explaining the FBI and Realm treasure trove than explaining his tagalong should he be stopped at Customs." Fred and Ted crack up.

"For fuck's sake, Fred. I don't want to hear another word."

"But it's such a good story."

"Fred!"

The dimpled detective laughs big. Really big! "How are Shelby and Amanda?"

"I had to get a doctor here for Shelby. She has a gash that required eight stiches, and an ostrich sized egg on the back of her head. Oh, did I mention the concussion?"

"Nope."

"Well, she has a concussion. Let's recap. The director of the FBI is down for the count, the FICA director quit, and the deputy director is dead and who the fuck knows where?"

Fred and Ted raise their hands, "We know."

"Shut. Up. While the doctor was here, he checked Agent Rhys' wrist which is sprained and wrapped. FYI, the story the doctor received was that the director and the agent slipped on an ice patch at the back door on their way in last night and fell onto one another."

"There was no ice last night," Fred reminds John.

"Funny thing, Fred, if you pour water outside when the temperature is below freezing, the fucking water turns to ice," John snaps.

"Geez, John, you need to chill."

"Not likely. I wake Shelby every couple of hours to see what her mental state is. The last time she was awake, she still had no idea how she injured herself or that we aren't a thing anymore."

The guys crack up and Fred adds on, "Well, the concussion gives her complete deniability about Jack McGovern's fate, which is good for her, and it gives you a reprieve from being out on your ass again, which is good for you. I'd say it's all good, John." Fred slaps him on the shoulder. "I need to check in with 275, do you think you can keep your woman happy for the next hour or so?"

"Not my woman, Fred."

"She's your woman, John."

Fred heads to Webber's basement and calls for an update, "Okay kids, what have you got on Osterman?"

Penny starts. "We've found connections to three former ranger veterans who live in areas where the female sniper visited during the past year. The Kid made quick work of getting Osterman's financials, including debit and credit card transactions and the money trail puts her in Wyoming close to veteran Blake Firestone, in Montana close to Chester Buckman, and in Pennsylvania close to Adam Noone. Firestone and Buckman work for franchise branches of Intestinal Fortitude, and Noone runs a privately owned firing range. All three are affiliated with nationalist organizations and crossed paths with Osterman and Reynolds in the Army."

Fred jumps in during the pause, "Randy, if you're about to go on a riff keep it in English."

"Will do, Tonto."

Fred jumps all over that, "Doesn't Tonto mean dumb?"

"Yeah, but I thought you'd be too Tonto to know that."

Penny ends the back and forth, "Fred, there are plenty of financial transactions for Osterman's time in Beaver Falls, the last one was at the end of July. Then, at the beginning of August, there's a thousand dollar withdrawal from a bank in Anchorage, then nothing for three months. Then, at the beginning of November, there's another thousand dollar withdrawal from the same bank in Anchorage. Then, activity begins back in Beaver Falls until the end of November. There's been nothing since."

"Airline flights?" Fred asks.

"Not under her name," Randy answers.

"Give me a minute." Everyone is quiet for a few, then… "Okay, I want a deep dive on the three ranger veterans. Start with Noone in Pennsylvania, he's more central to our action. If she's working on an elimination list she needs to stay close to her targets which means the East Coast. If she's not using her ATM cards, she's not using her own money. Osterman was most likely the one tooling around Drexel Hill in a cherry red Camaro. No question it was the car Benton Brettenvue boosted, and since he was on the run, he had cash in that car. It's hers now. When you're done with that research, see if there were any assassination killings in the Anchorage area during her three-month stretch there. If our assassin was in Alaska for that amount of time, she was doing something, let's find out what it was. That ought to keep you busy and out of my hair, Randall."

Penny chuckles her last words, "You know, Fred, you're part of this problem." She hangs up on the laughing man.

Fred finds Shelby resting on an Adirondack chair, staring at the Potomac when he returns to the great room. He joins her at the window.

"How are you feeling, Director Webber?"

"The banging in the head from the concussion has been replaced by an annoying pain in the ass," she says with a tiny smile and a look toward John.

"You remember?"

"I do."

"Good. That's good. Just want you to know, some of us will be out of your hair by the end of the day," Fred smiles as he steps away. He stops when she addresses him.

"Fred, when the RFI team leaves, make sure Maxwell exits with you."

"Yes, ma'am." Fred walks to John and slaps his shoulder, "Your woman remembers."

"Not my woman, Fred."

"That's what she said."

The RFI men are ready to vacate Virginia. They have worked a plan with Director Webber that Mike Monopoli and Amanda Rhys stay on as her security detail and that she work from home for the next few days. After a rousing back and forth of 'should we or should we not' deactivate The Realm listening devices, the decision is made that they stay live.

John was the deciding vote, "When The Realm figures out Jack is MIA and toss his place, they're going to spend some time and energy trying to find him. If we go silent, they might think we found out about the eavesdropping and took action against Jack."

Shelby turns toward John, the question of what happened to Jack is pushing hard. He turns away before their eyes meet and puts an end to the meeting before she asks the question, "Okay, let's roll."

Fred approaches Shelby on his way out. "Director Webber, Rocco Fiancetti will be calling you tomorrow to discuss matters. If you require immediate assistance, Mike can handle most things. If you require more senior level assistance, please feel free to contact me." Fred hands Shelby his card. "Take care, ma'am."

She sits quietly watching the sparkle and movement of the Potomac as she takes stock. "In the span of a few months, I lost Stacy Remington, my friend and the head of the FICA division, I learned my second-in-command bugged my home and office on behalf of a worldwide crime organization, I made a holiday trip to a forested fortress and came home with Caligula, my security was breached, my home was invaded, my life was threatened, and I somehow ended up with a concussion and stitches. As bad as all that is, I have no idea what happened when I lost consciousness." She stops talking at John's approach.

"I'm heading out. I know you won't, but contact me if you need me."

She nods but says nothing.

Mike approaches Shelby long after dark, "Ma'am, there's soup and your next round of pills in the kitchen. May I help you?"

"No, thank you, Mike. I think I'll just shower and go to bed. Please have Agent Rhys bring me my pills and leave them on the nightstand."

Shelby accepts Mike's hand up and leans into him until a sway stops. "Goodnight, Mike."

"Goodnight, Director."

Mike:	She's gone up for the night.
John:	Thanks for update.
Mike:	Where are you staying?
John:	Not far.

Ice chips and cold shoulders.

Felicity wakes to the sound of ice chips tapping her windowpane. The spot next to her is empty, the sheets, cold. She is flooded with a mix of relief and loneliness. She heads to the en suite and spends an inordinate amount of time in the shower, so lost in thought that she screams when the door is opened.

Mathis laughs as he steps in, "Not the reception I expected."

She pushes past him. He takes hold of her wrist and keeps her from moving forward, "What's wrong?"

"I don't know. Something," a memory flashes and she begins hyperventilating. The anguished mother pushes her back against the wall and slides to the floor, her arms wrap around her knees, and her face buries upon them.

Mathis shuts off the water and kneels next to her. He puts his hand onto her rapidly rising back, "Felicity, slow breaths."

She moans in deep pain, pushes his hand away and glares at him. "My twins," she sobs. "It's my twins' birthday."

Mathis tries to pull her up.

"Get out!"

He waits the hour it takes for Felicity to emerge. He is dressed and sitting in the club chair, his feet resting on an ottoman.

She glares, "I was hoping you'd be gone."

"Felicity, don't try my patience."

"Or what, Mathis, you'll hit me? No, you don't hit women. Or maybe you'll kill me. Please do, it will put me out of my misery, so that's a win for me, really. If neither of those suffice, tell me, Mathis, what will you do if I try your patience?"

The man removes his feet from the ottoman, stands in one smooth motion, walks out of her bedroom and out of her home.

It's late, she's physically exhausted and emotionally spent. She does not want to answer his call, but she has no choice, "Yes."

"Have you heard from Jack McGovern?"

"No."

"Call him and call me back," he disconnects.

Felicity makes three calls over the span of several minutes, then calls Mathis, "No answer, it goes directly to voicemail."

"He's in the wind. Webber fired him. His direct report in the surveillance division says every man on McGovern's team was put on a search for John Maxwell who quit the FBI and left Webber's house. Did you know any of this?"

"Not a thing. Has anyone been to Jack's place? Maybe he's hurt or something."

"He'd better be dead or something."

Felicity receives a video text as soon as Mathis disconnects their call. Her twins are straddling brand new bikes with training wheels, attached baskets, and handlebar streamers. The tots' helmets are fastened tight under their chins, still they flop a bit to the side when they wave to the camera. "Thank you, Mommy. We saved you a piece of cake. We love you, Mommy."

Felicity calls Mathis.

He ignores her call.

Holes in doors, not in heads.

Rocco is behind closed doors with Steve, who has returned to The Compound with an unusual guest and a shitload of questions.

"Tell me again why I had to sit next to a dead guy on a fifteen-hour flight that should have taken five hours tops, escort him to The Compound, and bury him in a grave that was prepared for your son, who is supposedly dead, but is currently pounding a track at the Athletic Center."

Rocco laughs at the Rambling One, "We couldn't call the U.S. authorities about Deputy Director McGovern's death because my entire team would have been stuck stateside being questioned for an eternity. We couldn't destroy his body because we need it as evidence in the event there's blowback on Director Webber."

"See, it makes perfect sense when you say it, Rocco, but I doubt the authorities are going to see things your way when they find out I smuggled a dead guy into Canada." He pushes from his seat, "If you don't mind, there's a long shower in my future. I need to get the stench of the stiff off me, and then I need to see Maura about getting the other stiff off of me." He laughs. "If you were Fred, you'd get the joke, Rocco."

"I got it, Steve."

Rocco is still laughing when he places a call, "It pleases me that you escaped the shooting, Shelby. Bullets are better in doors, si?"

She rubs her head. "I've been on the phone for ten seconds, and I haven't a clue about this conversation." She diverts. "Fred Serpico said you wanted to discuss certain matters. If the discussion concerns the shooting, I'm afraid I was unconscious for most of the event, so I'll need to do the listening."

"Si. The event and the fallout from it are handled, Director. I suspect The Realm has learned by now that you fired the deputy director, and when they enter his domicile they will find evidence to suggest he is on the run. Additionally, they will know John Maxwell is no longer with the FBI or with you." He pauses for her input, receives none, "I mentioned in an earlier conversation that John has a highly effective and unique skill set of filtering cases along a defensive slant. That is why you are alive today, Director. He did not explain details of the shooting before leaving your home. I will speak on his behalf. My former cyber defender, my friend, is on the streets as a hunted man with little to no protection. Maxwell lived for twenty years as an undercover agent for your Bureau, so I do not doubt his ability to stay one step ahead of enemy forces, but he is flying solo, which is never a good idea. The Realm wants him. We cannot afford for them to get him—that would be a professional loss, as well as a personal one. The nefarious ones already have one of our cyber huntresses; we cannot allow them to get our cyber defender." Rocco pauses again. This time, Shelby fills the dead air.

"Forgive my abruptness, Mr. Fiancetti, but I need to end this call. I've a splitting headache."

"Si, of course. When you recover, please contact Joy. She has made great progress in your research project."

Shelby loops the conversation several times, gets hopelessly stuck on one part, *Bullets are better in doors, si?* She leaves the sitting area in her bedroom and stands at a window overlooking the river. Bullets are better in doors, si? Bits and pieces start settling, she talks her way through the events before the world went dark. "Agent Rhys keyed the security pad, the security gates swung open, I stepped out of the car and stormed toward the Potomac, I turned the corner ……. blackness ……." Bullets are better in doors, si? ……. "I stepped out of the car and stormed toward the Potomac, I turned the corner ……. a door hit me ……. blackness. *Bullets in doors, si?*"

Shelby leaves her room, inches down the hallway, takes the stairs very slowly, and moves haltingly into the living room. She ignores Mike's request to stop. She presses her back against the wall and navigates slowly down the next set of stairs, stumbling down the last two. She pulls to an abrupt stop at the door that leads outside, pulls it wide, and stares at the screen door, "Bullets are better in doors, si?"

Mike offers her a hand, "Ma'am, you shouldn't be down here. Let me get you settled back upstairs."

She points to the head-high bullet hole in the door, "John hit me with the door."

"Yes, ma'am."

"I'd be dead if he hadn't."

"Yes, ma'am."

"Where is he?"

"I don't know, ma'am."

Snowfall Prison

Eli leaves bed to take a call, "Brother, it's been too long."

"Are you well, Eli?"

"Kuvianartok."

"You are not Inuit, speak English."

"I am happy, brother. Do we have our cyber defender? My huntress tires of inactivity."

"We will have Maxwell, soon. Some roadblocks need to be taken care of first. Someone is leaving," Mathis uses their code for a contract hit.

"Who?" Eli asks.

"Senator Morgan. My goal is for him to exit on January 20, 2020, exactly one year before the next presidential inauguration. Before I get into details I should update you on ……." Several minutes of updates pass before he circles around, "As for Morgan ……."

"Got it. I'll contact Osterman. Oh, shit. I need to go, Mathis."

Eli races to Leavy's room and finds her asleep. He grabs his laptop from the end table. It is still streaming the movie they were watching when he got his brother's call. He chastises himself for his momentary lapse then moves close to Leavy and touches her cheek. She moans but doesn't move. He kisses her head and leaves the room.

Leavy smiles.

Spares sure do come in handy.

Joy Fiancetti and Shelby Webber are on a very late call talking about a boy. They aren't really, but it sounds like it.

"He hasn't responded to my calls," Shelby laments.

"He probably has his phone off."

"He's pissed."

"You're talking about John Maxwell. He's always pissed."

The women laugh. Their jovial moment is cut hard by Joy's scream.

"Leavy is online—was online! Shelby, text John. Tell him Leavy is using her spare, and tell him to call me! He'll know what that means." Joy pulls open the Computer Center door and screams into the night, "Roccooooo!" In less than ten seconds, every armed person at The Compound is surrounding the Center with guns drawn.

Rocco pushes through the throng, "Gia, explain!"

"Leavy was online. She's using her spare."

The entire Compound erupts in cheers and tears.

Rocco gives them a minute to feel their relief and communal hope then sends them off. "Come, Gia, we have work to do."

John calls Joy. "Put me on speaker. How long was Leavy on?"

"Five seconds. She got on with her spare and typed Inuit. Hold on John, Rocco is putting Fred on speaker. Hi, Fred."

"On pins and needles here, Joy."

"Okay, I've got everyone on speaker. Let me repeat what's happening. Leavy popped online for five seconds. She typed one word, Inuit."

"Fuck. Fuck." Fred interrupts. "Penny and Randy are chasing Layne Osterman's trail, and as best we can tell, she spent three months in Alaska. She got money out of a bank in Anchorage at the beginning of August, had no other transactions until she debited more money out at the beginning of November. Within days of the second money transaction in Alaska, she was back in Beaver Falls and back on the money trail in Pennsylvania. She went off the grid at the end of November and hasn't used her bank accounts since."

"Joy," John interrupts. "I need to keeping moving. I can't sit in one place too long," tension burning his words.

"Go to Shelby's. She's off the ledge. You'd know that already if you answered any of her texts."

Fred and Rocco chime in, "Yeah, John."

"Oh, for fuck's sake. I'm out. I'll call you later, Joy."

Fred fills the silence left in John's wake. "Okay, Leavy is in Alaska, somewhere near Anchorage. No easy search ahead. Alaska is the size of Texas, California, and Montana combined. And Anchorage is the most heavily populated area in the south-central part of the state, but five minutes ago our search was worldwide, so this is good."

"You know an awful lot about Alaska off the top of your head."

"I lived in Seattle for a decade, Joy. If you live in Seattle you trek Alaska."

"Right, I forgot about that. Hey, Rocco, looks like RFI's got us our very own Yukon Cornelius," Joy jokes.

"Yukon, what?"

"Oh, for fuck's sake. I'm out. I'll call you later, Rocco."

Joy winks at her husband, "Was it something I said?"

"Ah, Gia, you delight me so."

"Hey, Rocco."

"Si, mi amore."

"Leavy is alive, and she's fighting to get back."

"Si. Let's help her get here."

Alexandria
John ditches his tail a mile from Shelby's house

then ditches his rental. He books it toward the waterfront place, runs through the tree line and breaches her security. He's inside her home within a minute of his feet finding ground. He pulls to a screeching stop at the sight of Mike's weapon trained on him.

"What the fuck, John? You couldn't call and maybe come in through the front door?"

"I'm being tailed. Didn't exactly have time for social graces. Where's Shelby?"

"In the great room waiting for you?"

"And Rhys?"

"In the gym."

"Join her, I want to talk to Shelby alone."

The woman in a pink cashmere cardigan, pair of jeans, and pink Birkenstock slippers turns from the bank of windows to face him. Moonlight over the Potomac softly backlights her golden, shoulder-length waves. "I'm very glad you're safe, Director Maxwell."

He crosses the room with an ease that's telling—of what, remains to be seen. "Call me John. I quit the FBI and no longer work for you. Did you receive a blow to your head that may have affected your ability to remember certain events, Shelby?"

"Yes, as a matter of fact I did suffer a concussing blow. That circumstance, however, has nothing to do with your current state of employment. You quit in a huff without submitting a standard letter of resignation or going through an exit interview with your superior," she smiles. "Until such time as protocol is followed, you are still the FICA Director of the FBI, I still outrank you, and I have a directive that I expect you to follow."

"And that is?"

"Hannah Leavy is in peril. She has provided a clue, and we are going to follow that clue. Director Maxwell, it's time to bring Leavy home."

"Yes. Director, there's one thing before I get to work," John pulls Shelby close and kisses her.

When she can pull air she whispers, "Welcome home, Caligula."

That's the ticket.

Senator Curtis Robert Morgan, of the great state of Georgia is standing on a magnificent wrap-porch at his estate on Skidaway Island overlooking Moon River. It's where he's spent most of his time since he returned from Lewisburg nearly a week before. The air outside is fresh and crisp, so too are his thoughts. The next Democratic Presidential Debate is nearly upon him, and he is ready, more than ready. He's been working his entire life for the moments he's living, but there is uncertainty in his future. The be all and end all of that uncertainty is who will stand as his running mate. Madison, his wife of nearly four decades, a brilliant political mind, is squarely in the mindset of a Morgan-Price, father-son, White-Black, experienced-eager, decent-decent Democratic ticket. The senator made the ask, now they need to see where Malcolm ends on the subject. Curtis is pulled from his thoughts by the touch of Madison's hand to his back.

"A penny for your thoughts."

"I'm afraid you have diminished the value of these thoughts, Madison."

"You are thinking of a Morgan-Price ticket?"

"I am."

"And?"

"It's a winning ticket."

"One worth a million or more pennies. Come inside and sit by the fire. There's nothing you can do here but catch a chill. It's up to Malcolm to make his way to the right decision."

Curtis reluctantly pulls himself from the river he loves and follows his wife indoors.

275

Gretchen stirs from her nap expecting to find Malcolm beside her. She feels his presence, but he is not near. He's across the room, his back pressed against a brick wall, his ass on the floor, his legs out straight, and his feet crossed at the ankles. His stare into space is concerning.

"Well this is new," she whispers.

"I need a talk, Woman."

Gretchen gets off the bed, checks DelRae, grabs a baby monitor, and follows her man to their conversation couch. Her heart skips a beat when he takes her hand and twines their fingers.

"There are some challenges ahead for me, Gretchen. The first is making it through this conversation without you edging in. I'd appreciate it if you'd just listen."

"Well, that isn't something that I'm usually inclined to do, but the look on your face suggests that—"

"Woman. Quiet. Please."

She nods.

"There is a groundswell for me to be Senator Morgan's running mate." He looks at his wife as though she should be saying something.

Gretchen tilts her head, "Are you waiting for my response?"

"I am."

"You told me to remain silent. Have you changed your mind on this, Malcolm?"

"I have."

Gretchen groans, "Oh, good Lord, are you going to be a flip-flopper politician because I generally do not support candidates who ride the centerline or bounce from side to side. Pick a lane, Malcolm, and stay in it."

He laughs at his woman, "I made a miscalculation, earlier. I want a give and take here."

Gretchen nestles her back against a couch arm, pulls her long legs up and organizes her thoughts, "Okay, the shear brilliance of this based solely on politics cannot be understated. I suspect Madison is behind this stroke of genius. I can rattle on about that, but let's flip the coin and look at the problems associated with this ticket because I'm quite sure that's your sticking point."

"Continue."

"A good swath of people are going to love the father-son angle, but the people who already don't like the Morgan-Price personal relationship will be reminded every day that they don't like this father and son. The hoopla over the salacious relationship between Curtis and Bertha is going to come around again, but if past predicts future, Curtis will weather the storm. As for you and Sage, your relationship with her is seen by most as a loving relationship, and in some respects I think people see you in a heroic light because you hunted Micky Strong down and made him pay for his crime. Now for Mama Girl. Things will get tough for her because of The Bus Company scandal, but she's been through the worst of it, I suspect. Then there's the racial piece, that's the significant issue with this ticket, though it shouldn't be. You know as well as I do that our country continues its struggle over race. Curtis and Madison have found their footing on this issue, although the two of them, side by side do not scream, 'he is White, and she is Black'. If you run with Curtis, a second interracial couple will take center stage, and this one has Gretchen Mitchell as the snow white wife of the biracial husband. That alone is a readymade reason for some to choose the other candidate, whomever it may be."

She pulls a very needed breath before continuing. "Having said all that, the Democratic party and much of the Independent voting block do not get hung up on race. They generally focus on policy issues. Curtis' voting record is strong, and your mayoral platform of education and environmental reform is much aligned to center-left and far-left voters." She takes a thinking breath.

"A negative for me is the length of time a politician has been in Washington. I'm a strong proponent of term limits, but be that as it may, I overlook this issue when need be and would ignore it completely when considering Senator Curtis Morgan as a presidential candidate, even if he were not my father-in-law. Huh, I don't think I've ever said those words. I like them. Anyway, his political tenure will be an asset on the debate stage, and his solid Democratic voting record should negate this issue for likeminded thinkers. Bottom line, Malcolm, after these past four years, it is going to be a jump ball," she smiles wide. "Yes, I used a basketball term," she giggles. "Look, people will either want more of the same, or they will want anything but the same. You and Curtis will give the voters a very good option. Yes, I'd say the Morgan-Price ticket is a winning one."

Gretchen hops off the couch at the call of their daughter, kisses the next vice-presidential candidate and calls over her shoulder, "You've got my vote, Malcolm."

The broadly smiling man stares out over Hufnagle Park where it all began, "The woman showed up out of the blue and said she needed a favor, and she hasn't stopped talking since."

Snowfall Prison

Eli Reynolds steps outside the log cabin to make a call. He purposefully leaves his laptop within arm's reach of Leavy.

The former agent knows the nearby computer is a test. "Eli isn't sure if I used his laptop the other night." She ignores the trap, "There's no need for me to do anything more than I've already done. I used my spare signature, and I gave the RFI team a cyber crumb to follow." Leavy nearly jumps off the couch when Eli returns. She was so engrossed in her thoughts that she didn't hear him enter the house.

"Good book?" he takes a hip on the couch.

"The best."

He reaches and closes the cover so he can read, "*And Then There Were None.* I agree, it's Agatha's best. Have you read it before?"

"Of course. I've read most of her works, but I saw a few on the shelves in the loft that I somehow missed."

"Let me guess. Hercule Poirot."

She throws a smile.

"I'm glad you're finding enjoyment, Leavy." As he walks away, she smiles wide knowing she passed his test.

You say blockbuster.
I say ballbuster.

Layne Osterman was just given her next mission, and it is big.

Sergeant Noone cautions the sniper, "You're going into the biggest mission of your life, Ranger. If you don't want to go out with the senator, you need to review your plan, execute each step, and keep your head clear. That means you need to get Eli Reynolds the fuck out of your headspace, Layne. When you're done with the senator, you should get the fuck out of the country for a while. Put some time and space between you and your handler." Sarge takes a seat across from her and demands her attention. "Osterman. Taking out a sitting U.S. senator is gonna bring the heat, and if you're too close to the fallout, you're gonna get burned." He sees the flash of stupidity cross her face, "Don't even think about going to Alaska or trying to find Eli. If the Feds or RFI are onto to you for the sniper kills in Pennsylvania, then they know about your trip to the Anchorage area. Stay the fuck away from there, or you will go down."

They spend a few quiet minutes: she, wrapping her head around the mission, and he, fighting his uneasy gut.

"I'm taking the senator out at his place on Moon River near Savannah. It's remote and difficult to access, but it'll be less guarded and emergency response will lag a bit. I'll be looking for a set up across the river from his home. Any thoughts?"

"Get your gear in order. Get your head on straight. Get to the location. Get the lay of the land, and then …....."

"Get the job done," Layne finishes the sniper's step-to.

275

Fred and Ted are in the Diving Center waiting on Penny and Randy. While they wait, they commiserate over their stalled investigation.

"Need a thread to pull, Theodore."

"And we need it fast."

The Betty Boop of the organization arrives with Penny and Randy, and deli sandwiches wrapped in parchment and tied with jute thread.

"Well, that's weird," Fred points to the tied lunch.

Peyton ignores whatever is going on and pushes in. "Ted, I have a question. When Patrol Officer Landry noticed the cherry red Camaro went missing, did he mention whether a different vehicle was seen on your street?"

All eyes swivel to Ted.

Fred jumps in, "Yeah, Poindexter, did the officer mention that? Because it sure would be interesting to know that sort of thing."

Ted leaves the Center, "Be right back."

Team members' mouths are full of ham, cheese, lettuce and tomato when Ted returns, "Black F-150 with Pennsylvania plates. Landry hasn't seen it for weeks and guesses it left the neighborhood around the same time Kelly Thompson was killed. ME ruled her death a homicide, by the way. The report says her death was the result of an up-close-and-personal break of the neck."

Fred pushes in, "Can't wait to find out how the dude in Layne's torched 2013 Chevy Tahoe met his fate. If it's death by shooting we may get ballistics. If it's an up-close-and-personal break of the neck, we've got a serial thing going on. Layne Osterman's a well-rounded, paid killer. She's got weapons and hand-to-hand battle options, and she's got an in-your-face mentality. So far, she took out two EMTs on an unfamiliar street and on a quick sniper setup; she took out a physical therapist at the woman's back porch with a quick snap of the neck; she tried to take out a pushy reporter inside a police detective's home; and we think she killed Tahoe Guy. She is skilled and ballsy. Question now, who's her next target?"

Ted and Fred mouth-maul sandwiches and guzzle drinks during the Penny and Randy Show.

"For starters," Penny begins, "there is nothing to suggest there were any assassination-type killings in the Anchorage area or anywhere in Alaska during the time period of August-November 2019. Keep in mind, we're looking at a trained assassin, so there may be victims who haven't been found yet. There are missing people from across the state, but they seem to be the standard fare runaways or spousal throwaways, not people affiliated with The world-domination-seeking Realm."

Fred jumps in, "Before we leave the topic of Alaska, let's do a dive on real estate transactions or long term rentals at campgrounds and cabins. Concentrate on south-central Alaska—it has it all, mountains, lakes, a national wildlife refuge, and a peninsula that's separated from the mainland. That area is surrounded by Cook Inlet and the Gulf of Alaska and has a ton of hiding opportunities."

Four sets of eyes and four raised brows turn toward Fred.

"Lived in Seattle for ten years and vacationed in Alaska for most of them. Why doesn't anyone ever remember that? Okay, moving on."

Randy stands.

Fred groans.

Penny admonishes, "Boys, play nice."

Randy begins. "No interruptions, Serpico. We started our diving with Adam Noone, a forty-seven-year old, never been married, father of two, originally from Philadelphia. The former sergeant was an Army ammunitions specialist who worked exclusively with ranger teams and had associations with Eli Reynolds and Layne Osterman. The sergeant owns and operates a private firing range named, High Noone, located in Penn Township, Berks County. The area is sparsely populated and very near Blue Marsh Lake, a National Recreational Area northwest of Reading. The manmade lake is managed by the Philadelphia District of the U.S. Army Corps of Engineers which provides him a whole lot of 'birds of a feather, flocking together' clients. Noone owns fifty acres of land, is financially solvent, has all necessary permits for his firing range and a clean arrest record. He dabbles in nationalist ideology and hangs a bit with survivalist groups, but he doesn't rally or publicize his affiliations. He has several vehicles registered to him; one is a black F-150."

Four sets of eyes turn to Peyton who offers a sweet, bow-lipped smile.

Fred claps his hands, "Okay boys and girls, Ted and I are heading to Penn Township northwest of Reading in Berks County, Pennsylvania. Continue researching what the hell Osterman was doing in Alaska. If there's anything that looks like a direct tie to Mathis or Eli Reynolds just make note of it. Don't go poking around and potentially tipping them off. You find something, turn it over to Joy for diving, and let me or Ted know. One last thing, Peyton Wells is on the books as a contract research analyst for RFI. She will continue her studies at Penn Law and will transition from research to legal once she gets her J.D. Both she and Randall will be heading to The Compound in May and will be there until September for extensive training."

Randy's smile is a mile wide, "Babe, didn't know this news, hell, I didn't even know my own news. Summer at The Compound, sounds like a blockbuster."

Fred shakes his head, "More like a ballbuster."

The Compound

Rocco joins Manuel and Doctor Weinstock in the gym. He's surprised at the progress his son has made since he's been on his feet. The doctor taps Manuel on the shoulder and motions him to head toward a set of bleachers. Rocco waves the doctor to join them. "Manuel, you will listen until I am finished."

"Oh, Jesus, another Fred Serpico."

Rocco laughs deep, "Son, I know my limits, I am no Fred Serpico, but I have important things to say and want to say them all. Leavy is alive. She reached out to Joy."

Manuel takes a seat on the bleachers near his father.

Rocco places his hand onto his son's shoulder, Gia saw Leavy online for a few seconds." He nods, "Ask the question that burns deep."

"Do we know where she is?"

Rocco shakes his head. "When she got online, she left a one word clue, Inuit."

"She's in Alaska," Manuel exhales his words.

Rocco nods, "There is more that leads us to that conclusion. Stacy Remington was killed by Paul Ferraro, and when he was incarcerated The Realm replaced him with a woman sniper named Layne Osterman. She spent three months in Alaska before being called up to the big leagues. Fred's team is making great headway in piecing together a road map of where she's been in the last year. Their focus is on south-central Alaska near Anchorage. Manuel, twelve hours ago we were searching the globe for Leavy, now we are searching a state."

"Are you finished?" Manuel receives a nod. "Come on Weinstock. I want you to push me to the limits. I've got a woman to find."

Rocco lets his son do what he needs to do, and when the time comes, the head of RFI will do what he needs to do.

Hammers, lists, and islands.

John returns from J. Edgar eager for a scheduled conference call with Rocco and Joy, but there's something that requires his immediate attention. He places a kiss on Shelby's lips, walks to a utility drawer in the kitchen, removes a hammer, grabs hold of her two briefcases and smashes the fuck out of the hanging zipper listening devices. Then he reaches inside and takes the two paperclip listening devices from the file folders and smashes the fuck out of them, too.

"There." He takes hold of Shelby's hand, "How are you?"

"At the moment I'm a little excited. What's going on?"

"We're making a conference call to RFI." The directors head to Shelby's home office. John places the call. "Rocco and Joy, are you on the line."

"Si. Go ahead, John."

"I spent the day diving deep into Turner Rodgers. I found a direct link between the presidential candidate and Felicity Ferraro, separate from her being his legal counsel. I'm gonna bullet what I've got, and we can dissect later. 1) Turner Rodgers has a Preston and Porter file floating in cyberland. When I decoded it, a client list fell out, a Felicity Ferraro client list." John ignores the gasps. "The listed names are encrypted, but Joy will crack the code easily. 2) There's a trail on a $500,000 wire transfer that begins in the U.S. from one of Turner's accounts, travels the globe, and ends up in one of Paul Ferraro's Cayman Islands accounts. That account is no longer in existence, but the trail still is. The funds begin their journey the day after Abigail Forrester's murder. If this is a payment to Paul Ferraro, aka Boston, for her assassination, then it looks like Senator Rodgers **personally** ordered the hit on Abigail and paid for it. 3) The fact that this money trail was tucked into a Preston and Porter file suggests Felicity Ferraro had a hand in the contract killing, perhaps arranging it with her now dead husband. It looks like Turner was keeping records for leverage against the Ferraro husband and wife team. 4) A scandalous tidbit was tucked inside this folder that may explain Abigail's leverage over Turner. The senior senator is sterile. He is not the father of his two sons. Face value, this seems personal and inconsequential stuff compared with world domination and shit, but keeping this knowledge secret from his kids was important enough for him to cede power to Abigail."

Shelby pushes in. "Or, the senator was desperate to keep the real father from knowing the truth."

"Are you onto something in particular, Shelby?"

"No, but I've definitely got a nudge going on."

"Work it later, Director. I've got more. I think The Realm is going dark. I didn't have a single tail today. No one followed me to or from the Bureau. I purposefully left J. Edgar three times to see if I'd pick up anyone. There was nothing. Keep in mind, I'm supposedly a hunted man. To test how hunted I am, I spent time outdoors and free-floating in cyberland. I didn't block my signature; I just went diving. I got some interest from Randy, but other than the regulars who tag onto me, there was nothing—nothing that would indicate The Realm has anyone tracking the preeminent cyber defender, the person they supposedly want in their clutches. If I'm correct about the organization going dark, there's only reason, and that's because it is preparing for a disbandment. What the hell do we end up with if The Realm shuts down? We don't know where Mathis Reynolds is, and Leavy's still missing and in the hands of Eli Reynolds. We don't have the names of The Arms. We don't know what The Realm was planning. We can speculate, but that's all it is, speculation. I don't know about you, but this feels like we're about to start chasing our tails and The Realm is going to be fucking dark when we grab hold of them."

Rocco is all over this question. "If that is the outcome, then the take away is that our investigation forced The Realm to disband. While they are down and out, we continue working. We have the client list of Felicity Ferraro. We break the encryption, find out who's on the list, and most likely learn who The Arms of The Realm are. With the correct pressure on these people we might find out what The Realm had planned. Further, we will have enough dirt to stop Turner Rodgers from becoming president, and get the upper hand against Felicity Ferraro, who might lead us to the Reynolds brothers. Most importantly, we will have focused time for hunting Eli and bringing Leavy home. I want Mike on 24-7 surveillance of Felicity Ferraro starting in one hour. There is no question in my mind that The Widow occupies a place of importance in The Body's organization and in his bed. If The Realm does go dark or disbands, I want her in our hands."

Dream maker – heart breaker.

Fred and Ted arrive at High Noone firing range at high noon. The first thing they see is a cherry red Camaro parked in what appears to be a private pull-off by the house. They scan for a black F-150 that isn't home right now.

"Incoming," Ted nudges Fred's shoulder. The men are approached by a thick man with a thick neck carrying a thick attitude and a big-ass gun that could easily take out a stadium full of people. "Haven't seen you two before," he gruffs.

Fred doesn't pussy around with this guy. He goes right for the thick necked jugular, "We're here for Layne Osterman."

Thick Man falters a tiny step, "That so?"

Fred nods.

"Haven't seen Layne since my active duty days—and haven't got your names yet, gentlemen."

Fred ignores. "That's Layne's cherry red Camaro sitting close to your house."

"That so?"

"Don't see your black F-150 anywhere, Sergeant Noone. I suspect we'll find it when we find Layne—and make no mistake, we will find her. And when we do, your ass is gonna be riding a prison bench with her."

Fred turns to leave and calls over his shoulder, "When you talk to Layne, tell her Fred Serpico and the whole Rocco Fiancetti Incorporated team is looking for her."

Sergeant Adam Noone calls over his shoulder, "We won't be talking until she's done with her mission, and you and your fucking RFI team won't figure this shit out until it's too late, Serpico."

Fred and Ted let their adrenaline out with a bunch of unanswerable questions as they speed back to Lewisburg. They stop at a greasy spoon and order a couple burgers and beers.

"Osterman's on a mission," Ted says while Fred pulls a long swig.

"I heard."

"You process any ideas on what that might be?"

"Nope."

"Any chance it's Penny?"

"Nope. This feels big, Ted. In fact, it feels like it might be the motherload."

Georgia on Her Mind

Layne Osterman is in the Peach State and singularly focused on her mission. She is deep into reconnaissance research, "The senator lives on Skidaway Island, which is a barrier island located in Savannah's Lowcountry twenty minutes south of the city. Senator and Mrs.

Morgan live in the oldest and most remote section of a gated community called River's Bend." While Layne does her research, she hums a bit of the Andy Williams tune she'd heard over the years, occasionally singing what little she remembers, "Moon River, wider than a mile, mmm mmm dream maker, heart breaker, mmm mmm mmm, going my way." She digs deep into research on the river that separates the Morgan estate and her vantage point. "The senator's estate sits on a narrow bend between the Skidaway and Vernon Rivers, well within my preferred sniper range. Mmm, going my way."

Her research complete, Layne starts out on foot—this part of recon isn't all fun and games. Though it's the dead of winter, there are plenty of trails and footpaths that get her to where she needs to be. She gasps at the beauty of Morgan's place and takes a few pictures of the Huckleberry Finn picket-fenced property. "Main structure with wide wrap-porch and nearby guest house. And looky here, the senator, himself." Curtis Morgan takes a few minutes on the porch staring out at the river, then walks a small path to the standalone house. "The senator is in residence," Layne whispers. She may not have her rifle with her, but she has everything else she needs. The Plan. "Very soon, Senator Morgan, when you step from your house and stand on your porch, I'll be here to put an end to your dreams with a bullet through your heart. Dream maker, you heart breaker."

Way *too late.*

Fred has been stewing a week since his return from High Noone at Blue Marsh Lake. There's been no sighting of the F-150, and he's no closer to figuring out the assassin's next move. He needs more than the windows in his apartment for effective processing, so he heads to Malcolm and Gretchen's great room banging on doors as he travels the seventh-floor hallway. "Meeting. Let's go!" The Pissed Piper and his band of followers arrive uninvited at the penthouse. The new mayoral family is enjoying a quiet moment on the couch when the motley crew appears.

"Listen up! I'm struggling through a process. Something big is in the wind—I can feel it. I just can't figure it out. Consider this a preemptive apology for my foul mood and disagreeable manner that is moments away. Playing catchup here for some of you. Sergeant Adam Noone, who lives in the Blue Marsh Lake area, let me know in no uncertain terms that Layne Osterman is on a mission, and it is the motherload. I need to figure this shit out before the female assassin hits her mark. Ted, ride our team until they find out what that fucking bitch was up to in Alaska while I try to figure out what that fucking bitch is up to now." Fred cools a bit and addresses Mama Girl and Faye, "My apologies for my language, ladies."

Mama Girl raises her hand, "Pish, don't worry about us son, you go get that fucking bitch."

"Mama Girl—" Malcolm begins and is cut off.

"Son, you learn to deal with a foul mouth from your Mama Girl from time to time."

"It's not the swear, it's the pish," he says, shaking his head in disbelief.

Mama Girl and Randy share shit-eating grins.

Fred claps his hands, "Mr. and Mrs. Mayor, I need to park my ass in front of this window. Don't know why. Don't care why. It's Friday, January 17. I expect I'll be here a good handful of days. Now, all of you get out and when you need to be in this area, don't talk to me. Out!"

Early on the third morning, Mama Girl finds Fred stretched the length of the leather couch by the windows, eyes wide open and fixed on the ceiling. She touches his face and he shoots up straight.

"Good, no need to call the county coroner. Get yourself in the kitchen, boy. And no talking back."

Fred does as he's told.

Mama Girl hands him a glass of orange juice, "Drink."

Fred does as he's told.

She hands him a bowl of cereal, "Eat. When you're done, get outside for some fresh air and into a shower for a fresh smell, then you'll right yourself." She turns and walks away.

Fred is on his second loop around and through Hufnagle Park and still thinking about Mama Girl. "Tough broad, bossy broad, gritty broad raising her son all by herself. Doing things no woman should have to do. Times were different back then, still Mama Girl was alone. Mama Girl was alone!" A memory bangs the fuck out of his head…

An energy pushed against Serpico and Xavier when they entered Abigail Forrester's condo. They pushed back against it as they moved about the first floor, eyeing this, thinking that, processing it all. Fred was in the kitchen when he called out to his partner, "Here's the legal pad that alerted Detective Brothers that this homicide needed to be kicked up the chain."

Manuel joined Fred and read the names on the pad, "Turner Rodgers, Benton Brettenvue, Topher Griffin, Penny Meehan, Jack Cane and ……. Curtis Morgan."

Fred hauls ass across the snow-covered park and darts across the street ignoring the blare of horns. "No. No. No." He slams his hand on the call button for the privacy elevator and jumps up and down impatiently waiting for it to arrive. "No. No. No." He throws himself out of the vertical ride and into the great room, startling Mama Girl. He races to the master bedroom and throws the door open.

Malcolm and Gretchen bolt from the bed, the disruption startling DelRae into a wailing.

Mama Girl takes the baby to the kitchen as Ted and the others scramble into the great room. "Granger, go to the bedroom! You, too, Ted!" Mama Girl demands. They arrived in time to hear.

"MALCOLM! CALL CURTIS. GRETCHEN CALL MADISON. THE SNIPER IS GOING AFTER THE SENATOR. CALL! CALL! JESUS, CALL!"

The senator's phone buzzes on the counter in his waterfront estate. Madison lifts the phone just as her cell starts ringing. She answers her husband's phone when she sees the name on the display, "Hello, Malcolm."

"MADISON FIND MY FATHER! HE'S IN DANGER!"

Madison rushes to the wrap-porch and to Curtis' prone form, "MALCOLM, HE'S BEEN SHOT."

"Fred, he's shot," Malcolm groans.

"Ted, Granger, call 9-1-1! Get help! River's Bend!" Fred grabs the phone from Malcolm's hand, "Madison, it's Fred Serpico, are you with him?"

"Yes."

"Is there a pulse?"

"Yes."

"Is he breathing?"

"Yes."

Layne Osterman doesn't know if she killed the senator, but she knows he's critically wounded, she's seen enough neck wounds to know Curtis Morgan won't survive for long. "It would have been a done deal if the man hadn't turned toward the house. Something called his attention making him turn just off center when I fired the round. He moved when he hit the ground—just a reach of his hand toward Moon River." She is on the main road by the time emergency response vehicles barrel-ass toward the senator's home. "Eli isn't going to like that it wasn't a clean kill shot, but even if Morgan survives, he won't be running for president, so the mission was a success."

The Body

Mathis is off the grid and off his game. He is reevaluating the state of things and the future of The Realm. He takes a legal pad, writes several headings, turns on a voice recorder, and begins dictating.

"Foundational structure: The Realm is nearly decimated. The Body is off the grid. Turner Rodgers is campaigning for president. Eli Reynolds is in hiding. Jack McGovern is on the run or dead. Financial structure: Realm monies are in offshore accounts in my aliases." He ponders a bit before addressing the next heading. "Disbandment pros/cons: Eli Reynolds, Turner Rodgers, Roland Gaffney and Felicity Ferraro know the identity of The Body. Rocco Fiancetti Incorporated team members know the identity of The Body. FBI Director Shelby Webber and John Maxwell know the identity of The Body. None of them will disclose my identity; they will continue their work, on the downlow and undeterred."

The flutter of gauzy curtains and call of sea birds beckons him outside. He steps onto a wide veranda, takes a long look at the surrounding beauty and continues his work. "Status of Realm members: **Eli Reynolds**—He wants Leavy more than he wants power. He has Leavy and the financial means to stay off the grid forever. Make him the scapegoat if necessary. Assessment/plan: no immediate retaliation against my brother. **Turner Rodgers**—He wants the presidency. He has enough information to hang me, but he would have to destroy himself in the process of destroying me. Now that his opponent has been neutralized, Turner may be seated in the White House. That's when I make a move back into power. He'll be desperate to hold onto the White House. In order to do that, he'll have to slip back under my thumb. Assessment/plan: no retaliation at this time. **Roland Gaffney**—Wants out of prison. He has enough information to hang me, Turner Rodgers, and the Gang of Eight. Assessment/plan: he's a threat that needs to be eliminated. **Felicity Ferraro**: She wants her children. She knows enough to bring everyone involved with The Realm to their knees. Assessment: pending."

The warmth of day and glare of sun cause him to remove his shirt and don a pair of shades. He takes another long look at the white sands, azure water, and cloudless sky, then stretches out on a chaise lounge. He continues his work. "RFI and FBI will hunt both Reynolds brothers, but it's me they want. Both organizations hunting me is too great a challenge. I need to rid myself of RFI. First step is finding the secret lair of

Rocco Fiancetti. Now, as for the Gang of Eight, they think Turner is The Body and Felicity is his underling. This group will want retribution for being deceived and being screwed out of their long term goals when The Realm goes fully dark and disbands. The Gang will go after Turner. He will silence them with offers of power within his administration. The threat to Turner and to me will be neutralized. The Gang will go after Felicity. She knows where their bones are buried. She'll be able to hold them off for a time, but she's a marked woman. Plan: pending."

Mathis gets off his duff and makes his way to the beach. As he moves, he finishes his work. "Action plan. Have the Realm go dark. Take out Roland Gaffney. Frame Eli. Build a new organization."

The Fall Girl

Felicity's hands shake as she reaches for the ringing cell. The tremble has been her constant companion since his last phone call. She answers with the only thing she can muster a single intake of air.

"Mrs. Ferraro, are you on the line?"

"Yes."

"The Realm is disbanded. You are the only one at the leadership level who is not free to move on."

The silence from Felicity's end is deafening.

"Are you still there, Mrs. Ferraro?"

"Yes."

"Good. This will be our final conversation, so please listen carefully. The obstacle between Turner Rodgers and his place in the White House is dead and will soon be buried. That ensures Turner's silence about the organization, its members, and its leader. If Turner is seated in the Oval Office a year from now, Roland Gaffney gets a pardon, which in turn ensures his silence. If by chance Rodgers loses his bid for president, both men will be dead within hours. As for the others: Eli will remain in hiding. An iron-clad file is being built to establish him as The Body of The Realm. Without Turner

Rodgers and Roland Gaffney to dispute the evidence against Eli, my brother will assume all responsibilities for the organization. Upon learning of the disbandment, the Gang of Eight will be out for blood. They will not go after Turner; they will, however, bleed you dry. That should be payback enough for you Mrs. Ferraro, but there is more. We will get to that later. Are you still with me?"

"Yes."

"RFI and the FBI will continue to hunt me, regardless of what happens with my brother. They know I am The Body, but after Turner and Roland are handled, there will be no one alive to help them prove their case—except for you. My adversaries had better not learn anything from you. Is that clear?"

"Yes."

"Is that understood, Mrs. Ferraro?"

"Yes."

"Good. Think back to the last time we were together; and we were having a tense conversation and you were trying to get a rise out of me. I warned you against trying my patience. You tried it anyway. During that exchange, you had a rather pithy question. Do you remember this event, Mrs. Ferraro?"

"Yes."

"Then you should remember your questioning words, but let me repeat them for you, '**Or what, Mathis, you'll hit me? No, you don't**

hit women. Or maybe you'll kill me? Please do, it will put me out of my misery, so that's a win for me, really. If neither of those suffice, tell me, Mathis, what will you do if I try your patience?"

There is deathly silence on Felicity's end.

Mathis breaks the silence. "I will do this." He ends the call.

In a matter of seconds, Felicity receives a video text. It shows a man's legs stretched beyond a low chair on a sandy beach that welcomes gentle rolling waves from a vast blue ocean. It is clear the man is recording the activities around him. The camera moves slowly, capturing images of four adorable children frolicking at the water's edge. They are slathered in sunscreen and have caked wet sand on nearly every part of their tiny bodies. Their giggles and squeals of delight lift to the world around them. Mathis calls out to the children, "We're making a video for Mommy. Say hello to Mommy and tell her you love her." The singsong voices of her children become part of a symphony of splashing water and calling birds. The heart wrenching sights and sounds continue for a minute.

The screen fades to black.

The End

More to come …

Please enjoy the teaser for my next book in the series,

Rebound…

REBOUND

THE GANG

--- PULLING THREADS ---

Book Fifteen

SHERYLL O'BRIEN

End line.

      Malcolm Price is in the grips of a nightmare. He's the lone Spur banging the boards at the AT&T Center in San Antonio, Texas. It's a championship game and there are no black and silvers on the court with him. There's no offense, no defense—just him. The point guard scans for his team as he toes for a jump ball. He abandons the search and runs his own game. The One locks himself in the key, fighting invisible opponents for shots and rebounds. He hears breathing, and the squeak of sneakers on the parquet, he feels the bang and push of bodies hard against him, but he cannot find anyone. "Where?" The sound of his pounding heart is deafening, sweat runs his face, stings his eyes. He swipes his arm across his forehead, runs his hands across his chest, his team jersey no longer there to dry them. He checks the scoreboard, the Spurs are losing by 2020 points, he is losing by 2020 points. He checks the stands for the man who can help him win. He wants that man to play the game with him. He fears he'll lose if he plays alone. "Where?" The player known worldwide as 77 takes a breather on an empty bench, dries his sweat, catches his breath, and does a frantic search of the arena again. He finds the man he needs sitting in the stands. **"Help me,"** he cries out.

　　The man stands and turns to leave, "You don't need my help, son. You can win on your own."

The battered man wakes from that nightmare—
　　　finds he's in the grips of another.

　　　　　From this nightmare—
　　　Malcolm Price will never wake.

ABOUT THE AUTHOR

She is not dead.

Sheryll O'Brien crafts characters without constraints. She tells them who they are, then let's them show her better versions of themselves. She gives them life and they live it beyond her wildest dreams.

Sheryll is a lifelong resident of Worcester, Massachusetts, where she is wife to the most supportive husband ever, and mother of two adult daughters, one who refuses to leave her home and the other who refuses to tell her where she lives. Of most significance, she is MammyGrams to the sweetest six-year-old, Hadley.

Sheryll worked several years in the fundraising community of Worcester County, writing grants for non-profit organizations. She began writing for her own pleasure after surviving brain surgery and breast cancer. Happily, for her fanbase of family and friends-—she is not dead.

If you have enjoyed reading my book, I would very much appreciate you taking a few minutes to write a review and post that review on amazon.com and goodreads.com.

The opinion of readers can help prospective readers make a purchasing decision.

To learn more, please visit my website, www.pullingthreadsnovella.com subscribe to my blog for updates on future projects.

I would absolutely love to hear from my readers, you can email me at,

pullingthreadsnovella@gmail.com

www.ingramcontent.com/pod-product-compliance
Lightning Source LLC
Chambersburg PA
CBHW070819180626
46818CB00001B/321